D0928023

Tin God

Flyover Fiction

Series editor: Ron Hansen

Tin God

Terese Svoboda

UNIVERSITY OF NEBRASKA PRESS · LINCOLN AND LONDON

*This book
is a work of fiction.
Names, characters, places,
and incidents
either are products
of the author's imagination
or are used in a
fictional setting.
Any resemblance
to actual events or locales or
persons,
living or dead,
is entirely coincidental.*

Source acknowledgments
for previously published
material appear on p. v.

♾

Library of Congress
Cataloging-in-Publication
Data

Svoboda, Terese.
Tin god / Terese Svoboda.
p. cm. —
(Flyover fiction)
ISBN-13: 978-0-8032-4331-6
(cloth: alk. paper)
ISBN-10: 0-8032-4331-6
(cloth: alk. paper)
1. Women farmers—
Fiction.
2. Nebraska—Fiction.
3. Fires—Fiction.
I. Title.
II. Series.
PS3569.V6T56 2006
813'.54—dc22
2005016912

Designed and set in
1550 and Minion
by R. W. Boeche.
Printed by
Thomson-Shore, Inc.

Acknowledgments

Big thanks to Sondra Olsen, Gay Walley, William Melvin Kelley, Gordon Lish, and of course to Steve Bull. Yaddo, The Bellagio Study and Conference Center, and the Writers Room also helped tremendously, giving me time.

Chapters 1, 2, and 3 were previously published in *Tiferet: A Journal of Spiritual Literature* 1, no. 3 (2005). Chapters 8, 9, and 10 were previously published in *Segue*, no. 4.2 (2005).

In memory of Bessie

Propter chorum

For the sake of the choir

Tin God

Chapter 1

Hi, this is God—G-O-D, God with all the big letters. And I'm out here in the middle of a field. Oh, yeah, I'm everywhere, duh. You can see Me anytime starside, whichever star keeps the quarks from going inside out, but right now I'm doing fieldwork, work in the field. In particular, I'm broadcasting like the granite man on top of the capitol building, the tallest in the state, the granite man whose hand casts out grain from a bag slung on his shoulder full of it.

Broadcasting. You thought electricity, a TV special via satellite, a Mile-High-Send-It-To-The-Sky? No. Grain. Remember, I put the Virgin Mary on the front of a box of cornstarch, no Indian maiden. The feather in her hair's a nice touch for those who recall the Virgin's exit, doves and whatnot in the jet stream. It's got to be grain for that girl. Corn, sorghum—you name it, I broadcast it, I seed it, it's all about grain.

It's not all about grain. It's grass too. Grass I care a lot about. Grass is what you have when you don't plant, but I plant that too.

You see, this field hasn't been grain, grain, grain, from King-dom Come, a season of soybeans, a rotation of rye. I'm talking pre-Interstate, pretrain, prewagon, pregrain, when grass grew by itself, just as grass. Up to here. And wind is what broadcast it then—meaning Me, of course—a wind that never stops, a wind that pets and fingers and searches the grass for whatev-er's lost—grain or what? Faith?

Dope.

I lay the grass bit on pretty thick.

I'm an impostor, of course. That's what the people who live in grass that high think and believing that keeps them look-ing around for a real god. Wind doesn't convince them other-wise, though goodness knows, I lay on plenty of that here. No light-handed broadcaster am I. But these people don't even sniff at wind, they have to have the incarnate, the usual meat, to make them mellow out and believe. Not that they don't al-ready have it in one Tall Pigeon Eye, but they don't give him the credit, he has a hard time of it. It's all about timing. Ex-cept for Me—I'm out of time, broadcasting whenever, a pre-tend impostor with no megaphones or ziggurats, though nev-er subtle. I say: You're going to end up dirt, then grass, what do you think? Timing is everything is what I think.

This is God, G-O-D. Add a W more and I'm broadcast-ing on the radio.

But who hears Me? The people living in this tall grass hear the wind and the grass together, but if I speak any louder they'll ask for a receipt, some sign and all, and that's annoy-ing in the end because, well, you know, I'm everywhere. It's all about expectation anyhow, about whether you're hearing what you've heard before. What these people in the grass don't expect to hear is the metal against metal on a man.

It's chunky chest-shaped-slabs-slapping-together-where-the-joints-fit-wrong time—that's what they hear but what they see is a big metal bug, face down in a fold of all that tall grass, stirring against a metal hat wedged sharp edge down into the earth, the head of a man pinned in its cup, the head jerking up against it.

Now these grass people are just out for a few days' hunt, the ladies and the dogs being left behind, but they are hunger-driven as always, and also out-of-the-village rowdy, with bets on who will find anything fit to eat first.

It is Tall Pigeon Eye who finds this vision of metal bug by tripping over the same pea vine as the metal-hatted man and falling hard into the same press of grass that he still holds down with his bulk. Tall Pigeon Eye is not my most graceful incarnate nor my smartest. Perhaps this is a result of an unfortunate drop he encountered at the time of his, as it were, birth, that is to say, when he was cast out of a cloud over a nice stretch of grass just after lunch, that meal no one makes much of midday here if there's really only sleep to be had, and that's the way it is with people who live in grass, not much lunch and a drowsiness that comes over their brains because they're being touched by sun straight up, a drowsiness like a cloud.

It was a warm and hungry lunchtime when Tall Pigeon Eye arrived. He didn't force himself through the forehead of some big shot or emerge squalling as the illegitimate foal of a local lady of virtue, but chose instead to set himself down out of an actual cloud into the grass, the sun full blast everywhere but there, so not too many people in the grass noticed his moment of arrival until he fully jettisoned down with a bump.

It is irritating that these people celebrate the least nuance of rabbit warren occupancy but not the splendid, gold-lined arrival of a decent-sized cloud with an incarnate on board. He should have made the day stormy—that they keep an eye on. Anyway, one or two of them looked sharp, having heard a thump and a cry of pain, the noise almost enough to account for a stranger showing up. When they ran toward the sound, they thought meat, lunch, which is after all, the incarnate's purvey by definition, and held disappointment foremost when he was located, and wondered. He had to come from somewhere. No one thought, Check the cloud. His odd, fixed look—the result of the drop on his face—lent him a touch of stranger credibility, and he wasn't nude, he had done his research. They had a name for him right away, a name that he heard as soon as he hauled himself up, swaying and grabbing for a handhold in the sharp-edged grass, his wide flat bum coming up against the face of somebody who had until very recently been asleep but on seeing the bum, a truly flat bum I'm afraid, another result of the fall, and with Tall Pigeon Eye turning his fixed eye on him, the eye yet another souvenir, turning it to have a look at whomever it was he had landed so close to, and his neck stuck out, turning, eyes popping, and well, that man laughed and called him Tall Pigeon Eye and Tall Pigeon Eye said, Yes? and the man and the others clapped him on the back and offered him what lunch there was, the way they do.

Of course I gave Tall Pigeon Eye cover, knowledge of family. Black sheep are handy for this, the Aunt Jane and Uncle Rupert who choose exit and are not accounted for in the mumbling of begats until someone shows up to claim them as kin and a free meal. Later on there's all this business with

Social Security numbers and credit ratings—it's quite messy to launch an incarnate today. Still, you'd be surprised what you can do now if you show up with cash.

Ah, god/gold.

I usually lose touch with an incarnate once he puts himself down. Father, father, why hast thou forsaken me? A lot of community outreach has to happen to get things going for him, a lot of courting without conception, and, despite the jolliness of the early years, a dreary solemnity has to replace the Las Vegas wit to keep the legend moving along. Who remembers an incarnate's jokes? God's, maybe. By the time Tall Pigeon Eye stumbles again, this time into the man with the metal hat, he has standing but not belly laughs, he has people who owe him.

The man stirs.

You never know how people will take to seeing someone who's not just like themselves. In my experience, the ones who get along, they watch what comes along, they're cautious. You only have to have a few of your kids turn black and die from a handful of mushrooms nobody studied to get the idea. This group puts one berry into their mouths and then a sprig of something else and then another sprig—to counteract every possible poison. That's how spice got to be. But no one's written that up yet, how spice and life come linked so close.

Hey! says Tall Pigeon Eye, pulling himself back onto his feet. The others, bored, beating the grass for game in the casual manner of late afternoon, take an interest, circle back.

They collect.

The choice for these grass people is: wait to have a look at this metal-wrapped creature, or kill it. After all, they are out on a hunt, they've been singing, Kill, kill, kill, since noon. They don't rush up like they did to Tall Pigeon Eye, and give him the high five, that's for sure. For one thing, Tall Pigeon Eye showed up in an outfit that matched theirs. They come to a halt in the thick of the grass and start to whisper about this metal man, about what kind of trouble he must bring, and what kind of man.

The man rolls over on his back, the metal hat falls off.

They, with their no-beard look, whisper a little louder about the wisp on his chin hanging on like a badly attached rag, about his fingers that spasm, about his size relative to theirs which is big, about his skin which is mottled—their color and lighter—with dirt. And about killing.

He opens his eyes.

They snap their mouths shut, they whip back farther into the grass, you'd better believe it, whip off like mink from a fire.

I have not been generous with blue eyes in this place full of grass. You'd think with all the sky on top spread out so blue and cloudless most of the time that I would be inspired to blueness in the genes now so lovingly replacing what used to be called God's will. But no. Black is what they get. I forget why.

The man's eyes are blue.

God, they gasp. Whatever. They always name Me something short, like a pet that needs to be called a lot. Spot! Spot!

Now, Tall Pigeon Eye is my man-in-command, the incarnate moment, the flower that has fallen, the bang on a can. He's well aware of who has been foreseen and dreamt of and talked to death of—and it's not Tall Pigeon Eye. Timing is everything when it comes to a god. And sometimes different color eyes.

No eyes of blue for Tall Pigeon Eye. He wanted to be discovered for himself, he wanted his godship earned. Every incarnate has his schtick. He is in fact, color-blind, the way he feels every incarnate is supposed to be. But by the end of his life, he's all-out blind and falls into a well and befouls it. It will be after he's finally made some reputation for himself as a fixer-upper of broken limbs and barren women with just a glance, more or less. Sometimes he used stinky green sap or he spooked people, and sometimes with barren women, well, he took matters into his own, as it were, hands. This is not good, but what can you do? He ends up in that well on account of one of those tuppings, sperm on a stick is what it is, he gets a push into that well he can't see but still, despite his drowning and decaying, he keeps them coming back for more, for sips and vials and gallon jugs of his essence. While the native populace is being killed off by the next soon-native populace, whole shipfuls of that well water he's steeped in is sent back from whence that populace came, along with testimonials on the fecund power of the well, but said three ships sink, boom, boom, boom.

Even an incarnate needs luck.

This man, the one they're calling god, is not good luck for Tall Pigeon Eye. He glances up at the sky, and I see his scowl. What does Tall Pigeon Eye want? Angels with banners covered with directives?

God, the others say all together.

Wait a minute, whispers Tall Pigeon Eye. That's not Him.

God/Spot/God/Whatever. They drag Tall Pigeon Eye farther back into the grass. Not so loud, they whisper. At the sound of the dragging, the man with the blue eyes hunkers up on his haunches and though he can't see too well now because he's been out for some time, he sure hears all that whispering, and this makes him think he is gone for good, the grass and its whispers closing around him like a wave he can't see the top of.

He closes his eyes.

He's bleeding, whispers Tall Pigeon Eye, checking his own hand for wounds. Does god bleed?

Blood does wriggle out from under the metal hat the man's resettled on his head. A curl of it runs straight down over the side of his head.

You'd have thought a chorus of Man, Man, Man would have come in to support Tall Pigeon Eye right then and there but no, the blue eyes open up a second time and suck that chorus right out of them all but Tall Pigeon Eye, especially since the blue eyes are not focused so well and look so wild, as wild as a god's playing over that grass, the grass leaning down on him so close that it could be the grass that whispers about the blood.

The man is wild. He has been on a horse three days straight, peeing off the side and holding his bowels, so deathly afraid of the grass is he, like all the rest of them, the ones who ride on ahead, who don't see him fall, the ones who go on into the grass so fearful they don't even turn around. Like them, he's been afraid of this ocean of grass, this rough-weather tsunami of grass that messes and fronts the wind in a boil, my wind, this grass that grows so high those who have gone ahead talk about putting a boat on it, conjoining the wind the way they've done with water where serpents haven't yet caught them, where something as non-serpent as a plant, well, a slithering pea-plant, lassoes him at last in amongst that fearful grass.

I do get carried away to the rhetorical side, wanting the words to sweeten themselves, to chip thought down to stone tablet brevity and then try for the purest. Well, sometimes it comes out clipped, and sometimes it comes out clipped and long, which is how speech happens for god.

Anyway, this fear of the grass reaches into him and squeezes his face about off so all you really see is the eyes.

Those blue eyes. The whispering ones in the grass figure they have at last caught themselves a god, they have captured one but now what? To their credit, they resist what most men do when faced with the chance of being less than what they have caught—they watch, they do not kill.

Tall Pigeon Eye shrugs.

Dios mio, the man says to the grass and lunges back into it.

Chapter 2

This is a mess, says Jim. He removes his Feed and Seed cap, he puts it back on. He stretches his neck way up over the steering wheel in the hope of seeing at least one corner of the field not mown down by hail and rain and wind. He stares at the dripping sorghum, its big purple heads laid over or shoved up, a whole section's worth, folding and heaving, all eight feet tall of it confused, mile after mile, where the twister touched. I hope I bought enough insurance to cover it.

You're worried about a crop? A bunch of vegetables? Pork hyperventilates, beating his ringed hand against the front of his silk shirt. What about insurance for the bag? I'm going to need real insurance.

He cracks the car door to have more air to suck.

No sweat, we'll find it. Jim puts the truck into park and gets out to wade in the ditch runoff.

Pork looks down at the suede of his shoes. I think the wind

took it, he says out the window to Jim's back. It's probably scattered all over.

Maybe it did, maybe it didn't, Jim says, sinking in mud. That bag was pretty heavy.

Pork shoves his door wide open, sits sideways in the seat before he takes his own step into the mud. You had to throw it.

You had to drive your black Porsche, a real flag of let's-do-a-deal. Why, that cop would have been foolish not to speed up to check us out. I mean, really. Jim uproots a stalk to look at the damage to the root, or to damage it, he can't decide.

I'd kill myself if I drove what you drive, says Pork, lifting his feet where they keep sinking, looking around.

That was some wind, says Jim, tossing down the stalk.

Torn-up plants play in what's left of the field, leaves wave. Already a little dust whips itself up out of the mud.

Who knew? says Pork.

The radio knew, everybody knew, says Jim. You can't complain about that. He lifts a thick pile of the beaten and bent sorghum and puts it down quickly when it starts leaking stink. He wipes his hand across his Pink Gnees t-shirt. You were in a hurry.

Maybe the buffalo ate it, says Pork.

An animal eyes them far off in the next field, large enough to have eaten a nearby haystack.

They're crazy anyway, says Jim. And evil. But that bag would have had to fly.

Buffalo walk. They even run, says Pork. I've seen it on TV.

Jim bends to check out more root. Six feet of the plant springs up but not the grain-bearing head, which still wags low.

Two steps later, Pork says, Oh my god—there it is.

He picks his way double-time over to where a bulging plastic bag inflates with wind, snapping alongside a downed stalk. Goddammit, let me just—

He tries to extract the bag whole from the mud and trash that it's mired in but fails, and his hand comes away with just half the plastic and all the mud.

Jim walks up behind him. That's not it.

Yeah, says Pork. I know. He lets the torn plastic fly.

There's a lot more bags here. Jim points to a couple of others caught against the fence. Sometimes I think Safeway's doors stick open when the electric goes out. He gestures toward a facility how far away?

Great, says Pork.

Look, Pork, you're not in the slammer, right? I got the stuff out of your car in time, right? Jim is slow to annoy but the crop's like this and Pork is truly bellyaching.

You've got to help me find it, Jim, wails Pork. I do not have much time.

You're just lucky it's in my field. Jim looks past him.

Pork makes his way toward a matted corner. He considers it, then yells: We had just about ditched him when you had your good idea to toss it.

Hey, you didn't even get a ticket, Jim yells back, shaking his head as if that was an oversight. I did the right thing, the only thing to do, considering. And I know exactly where I tossed it—right over there—

He points to an area not too far from the stretch of fence near where Pork is headed that is bare as bone. But as to where it has gone—he shakes his head again.

Pork looks away from the fence and up into the sky, which is perfectly blue now, its armada of black cloud having floated right off the curve of the earth an hour ago. It has to be here somewhere, he says. It's as big as a brick.

He puts his hand up to shield his eyes, to help him look farther, turning in his waterlogged shoes, *schlurp, schlurp*, in a circle. Jim does the same. The two of them end up looking at each other. Jimboy, says Pork after they laugh, look at that.

A couple of rabbits have come out to hop at his feet.

Maybe they have it, Pork says.

Right, says Jim. They mistook it for a head of lettuce and hauled it down their holes with their big buckteeth.

Pork looks at him in true pain, the pain of someone who finds it hard to laugh when he should. Maybe we ought to drive all the way around to start with. To check the fence.

Jim nods, head up, head down.

I could really use some drugs, says Pork. Right now.

They didn't have farmers when I started, nothing official I mean, with bailouts and forms to the government twice a week. Mostly women saw to it. Now there's chemicals and mortgages-up-to-here or the soul, whichever comes first—to pay for all those enormous machines that cut or clean or seed or reap. Even the grim reaper's reaper, the first implement I ever really took an interest in, sits around in junk-turned-antique stores now, expensive like all the rest of the stuff.

But I still help the plants rise up out of their leached land, out of land that's bug-infested or droughty or chemical-soaked or mostly blown away. And then what do people want?

Meat. Not the incarnate anymore, no, not him, just a thick slab of steak, please. And no vegetables. Ever see an advertisement for a carrot? Not many, and none for whole grain. A few whale-watch people, you know, the ones who buy rubber shoes with spikes that torture the soles—they eat whole grain treble-priced. Meat is what mostly goes inside those plastic bags that catch on the barbed wire or flap on telephone poles where the footholds still stick out for linemen, plastic bags that ought to be for packing my wafers or boxes full of something better than meat. Not that these two are interested in what's good for them. Golden calf, my foot. What they want comes plastic-wrapped and stamped purple: Inspected Grade A coke.

I'm out in the middle of my field now, broadcasting here and there where the crop's lifted off completely, trying to spread the seed and squeeze the kernels—such as they are after that tornado. It has hosed this field into a mess, that's for sure, the way when you squirt water at high pressure and plants blast out of the way in every direction. God's penis, some of the sex-bound call it, dragged across the field until the dirt clods harrowed up to make the rows writhe and long stalks slither against each other where they're not supposed to. This is how it looked when the grass grew up to here—over your head—with all the rows peripatetic, willed and wild and tall. It grew thick this time of year and not in rows. No, you couldn't see out anywhere, so tall and thick was the curtain.

Thick with praise for Me.

Thick and tall because I said so.

People don't want the incarnate these days, oh, no they don't. There's insurance problems to start with. First of all, a

15

god falls into a well and then what? They don't bottle it like they used to. Or look at Mohammed, insurance adjusters go crazy when I mention him, another disappearing trick, here and then not here, and causing a lot of translation problems, not to mention terror. Or Elvis and his ride. No, I've decided to come down this time and do myself as myself. Grass roots, that's the ticket, get them where they plow. Fieldwork. Broadcasting.

I'm as dazed as anybody else after my break of four frosted, creme-filled chocolate donuts, when a black car stops at the end of the fence and a young man in a girl costume— what they call soft shoes around here and shirts that have to be dry-cleaned—gets out on the passenger side. He's from outer space: hair as long as the Sacred Hearts that light up in the back of car windows, earrings, pants that reflect, a tattoo on the back of his very brown—more than a tan—neck. And black eyes to boot against that skin, fluoresced a little they're that dark. The other wears the usual bill cap emblazoned with a company stamp, filthy jeans, and a t-shirt crossed with advertising. Those two.

Excuse me.

Yeah?

Did you see a plastic bag?

Not a one.

Strange, says the tattooed one. All the other fields in the neighborhood have lots of bags in them. Quite a number since the tornado.

I can see that from your backseat. A pretty good catch you got there.

Well, says the other, mind if we look around?

No, I say. I give them my curious side: What's in this bag you need so much?

The two of them look straight at Me as if they have not thought of need. It had chopped meat in it, says the one who wears the weird clothes.

I'll tell you what, if I find one with meat in it, I'll give you a call.

Thanks, says the other. That'd be great. But he looks around Me as if I'm standing between him and a heaven of plastic bags.

Say hello to your dad for me. Hardy, Senior, right?

That's him, yeah. I'm Jim.

We shake hands, then he searches the sky as if his name is written up there in lights with a finger pointing to it. He's shy outside of his age group.

And you, you don't look so familiar, I tell the girl/boy. Could be you come from Denver. Or going to.

I got to go, says the Denver boy. Thanks. He gives Jim a look and hauls open the side door of the car.

Right, says Jim, and nods. It was just an idea. Nice to see you around, he says to Me, just the way his dad would.

I took a few months off, I tell him. You can do that if you just have grass. I shake his hand again and then lean toward the one with the earring, the one I know well enough was born and bred pre-soft shoes in the neighborhood, and I shake his too.

They both get back into the black car and sit in it like they mean to wait Me out. After I give them a little wave and don't move, they drive real slow on the wrong side, no one coming for miles mind you, both of them hanging out the windows.

Cute, but I have better things to do.

Chapter 3

In the flesh he's hardly the five-o'clock-shadowed swarthy hero they put on a ship for six months and then clap on a horse to go out and discover ignorance. He is the ship captain's nephew, and he owes the captain because he lost the captain's gold—a big part of it anyway—and his lease on the back twenty no one knew about in Madrid when there were lots so big you could forget them. He lost it all on a road between two *cuidads* at home, traveling among oaks that folded themselves over and above his horse and the horses of men heavy with the latest in crossbows who rode with him so he wouldn't lose it. He was set up somewhat, the idea for him to head up the gold run was a rival's, a guy who wanted his place in accounting, who made it seem that this was going to be his big break, this sitting in a saddle all day a nervous wreck under all these overhanging oaks, to be finally congratulated with a grunt at the port. He certainly didn't get the grunt.

The rival made mention of the convoy to men who hide in trees that hang over horses, and they did swing down with their swords onto the necks of the men all armored except at the back of the neck where their shoulders meet, where their swords went. After a biff and a stab and then a cut on the hand of the man in front who said, Yes, take it, take even the papers to that back twenty, who held out papers with seals on them which mean money to everybody, until those men falling out of the trees were happy to take them too.

He was that man in front of course. What was he supposed to do? Fight unto his death? Even as his life flashed before him, even as he saw his men's lives flash before him, dying like that over gold seemed extreme. For gold? Really? His practical side, the one that had elevated him to chief accountant at such a tender age, thrust itself forward, totted the odds and the rewards. He considered what else they might want, what might leave them satisfied and in a hurry to get away.

He dismounted, thrust the reins of his horse into their hands.

Nobody had devised repayment plans back then, other than execution, other than going along on the ship as a hand. They called it indentured, which sounds as if it has to do with your teeth, but it mostly means by the skin of your teeth you get your life back later. Maybe.

He hadn't even a metal suit to wear until they were out of the boat and well into the expedition, far into the search.

You know the search.

Gold is just a misspelling of god. G-O-D. Got that? The *l* is wrong. These men he traveled with would do anything for just a tiny bit of gold—dust even, dust that does not rust or decay—like God.

Not being a volunteer and feeling the way he did about gold, that is, preferring its enumerative rather than its emotional draw, he wasn't as addled by the long march for it as the rest, but after a while being with those who worship really does make you want to worship too. He was coming around to the idea of gold/god when he fell. What else made sense? The brains of the men in metal were fried and refitted with the sun—which was gold. It didn't take long across this land, land, land to bow to the gold god, a god whose face you couldn't look into. And what does gold that bright promise? Like all gods, it promises everything.

Well, I hadn't promised everything to the guy who had worn the metal suit before him. He died of fever in his sleep at the three-week mark, on the march they were making to a whole city made up of the stuff. The suit stank by daybreak and the man had to be gouged out of it like lobster from the shell quick after the heat-swelling set in.

This man with his blue eyes was the gouger. He needed that suit or he knew he'd soon be meat like that man, the rest of them ready to kill each other in their worship of gold at the first glimpse of any city made up of the stuff, all of its gold already wagered and spent. At least he was wising up to protection, claiming that suit for himself.

I haven't said what his hat is made of. It is regular metal but an experiment of the man who had died. That man had it tinned so it would not rust, so it would shine with whatever glory the sun gave out in this new place, a kind of gold only not quite so gaudy. He couldn't afford silver. Many others marching or riding beside him, but especially marching, wanted the hat, many others had baited him with their unfound gold goods because it shone and flashed against that sun so well and true it could have been as good as gold if tin were just a little more rare.

But not many will gouge. They let him have the hat too.

Whether a whole city is in fact made out of gold I won't say, but there is afoot some blasphemy about paved streets from people who swear they've pressed their lips to its gold stones. As a tease, I keep moving that alleged gold spot around. First here, where the sun flashes on every swag of grain, then to one of those inland seas with salt shores, then onto a wedding cake of sponge and coral in the middle of the Pacific. You've probably seen a gold city yourself over the head of your dog hanging out of the car window at night and thought, Gee, there's a town that's not afraid of paying for lighting. Several times several men have darkened such a city's aforementioned paving stones with their blood. And once a woman, quiet in a canoe, having eaten most of her mate on the long voyage after she had had his seed, saw the place but didn't stop.

I like that, god/gold.

So when the swelling starts on this lost man while he's lying in grass this high under sun so hot, with Tall Pigeon Eye and the others whispering in the nearby grass, he sheds the suit himself. But why does he swell? He has had no food, no water, he's not sick like the last man, nothing is broken.

Fear swells sometimes. He hears the whispers and it's not wind and it's not grass and it's in no language he knows, if it is language and not just loose tongues in the grass—the shaping of the air—and he fears. Then the sun goes behind a cloud and he hears the whispers swell too, like his skin against the metal, like the fear.

He sheds the armor—but not all of it, not yet.

He drags himself forward, still on the ground, and turns neck first, then he drags his body forward again, and turns again. To take the armor off here, with whispers between the stalks, whispers in the air?

He slams the side of his head with his hand.

The whispers rise in sound, rise like birds disturbed, birds that have swooped overhead all day and now leave to settle somewhere in trees—or more grass.

Slamming his head makes no difference at all to his hearing. The whispers are not in his head. That's good. He doesn't hit himself again. Instead he stares at the grass and feels his flesh swell.

He must take off the armor. It is close, too close. His breath comes quick as if the armor tightens around his lungs, then as it does. He unbuckles it at the worst of its seams. Since the armor was not made for him, it doesn't fit at all, it chafes, and he has a running sore on his skin near his waist that won't heal. He ties thick wool next to the unhealed skin at the break in the armor, so the armor won't cut him further if he turns in his sleep, if he sleeps in this grass that makes him afraid to take it off, this tall thin grass, but he doesn't take the armor off yet. Instead he reaches for his hat.

While he gets a grip on his hat, he runs his hand over his cheek and scrapes off dried bits of blood.

Up to then, like all young men in all grass, he is immortal, a kind of god, though he doesn't preen and strut like others do, not even in the very face of cholera and blackwater and still not dying. Starvation has loomed big against this immortal stance too, especially on a trip this long with not enough luck. But he hasn't starved yet, though for a young man he does suffer thin hair—is this from the hat? The whisperers whisper about his fine wrists—useful really only for totting up sums inside lace cuffs is what they don't realize—and there's that wisp of beard, which either means he's too young for much growth or it's related to the hair-on-head problem, a hairlessness or an illness, or he's mad, say the whisperers, because they would never, in a thousand years of fashion, be caught dead with hair on their faces. They pull it out. He has indeed been pulling out his beard but not to improve his good looks. Having seen roaches climbing into the hair of others in their hammocks on the ship, roaches that pull out the hair for their nests, he wants to get rid of the beard hair before the roaches get it.

It isn't the helmet that's doing it.

He does preen a little then, they all do, each in his own way. They all think they're the immortal Me, center of the strut and the struttee. But not now. He brushes off the blood and looks around like he means to go on anyway, despite his horselessness, on to where he was going, to push his way back to the rest despite the grass sea he has fallen into so suddenly and lain so long in already, despite his fear of it. He stands and staggers, then walks right into the grass.

The whisperers gather themselves.

He's glad to have time off that horse anyway. And a nap—the others will envy him his nap. They'll call him a lucky sucker and give him the heigh-ho and a slap on the ass. His horse will whinny as if it were none of her fault, and he'll launch himself back up on top of her, rueful—but napped. Now he follows the sun, which follows the crushed grass through the grass.

It is not crushed for long. See how the wind works at the tips, brushing them back and forth, coaxing the stems up to where it's most convenient for chemical exchanges to occur, where the stalks don't break at the bottom and soon stand again, one next to the other, having forgotten their bending, their being gotten out of the way?

Although the sun still shines its burnished shield (we can wax a Homer here, given the shield is put forth—and not gratuitously—as emblem of god in gold, gold in sun), the sun will soon lean low a lot sooner than the man thinks it will. He had lain there long. But where the sun is doesn't matter to the man now, it's still time for him to go, to get going. Some time is lost, that he knows, he's afraid to know how much, his horse could be so far away. He pushes hard and quick into the grass, he wrestles past it as if he expects dinner and a bed just beyond it, as if it were just a curtain he has to pull back to see where those ahead of him have laid out stones for him to follow or, at the very least, to find the left-behind droppings of a horse or horses.

Before, his horse let him see over the grass. Now the grass is a box with sky for a top, a tight box that the wind refits every minute, where maybe horses have passed except that the wind pulls the grass up quickly from wherever it's bent from their hooves, and what they drop small creatures consume with fervor in and out of their holes. So there's mostly just grass and no sign, no way out of the box but up.

But he's not bothered by that problem or he's in such a hurry he can't be. He has to catch up, and the men he pursues will soon have to halt too, or have halted, and he will push through to where they sit, eating yesterday's mush with the crunch of dry berries and slapping their thighs with laughter at the joke of his falling off a horse, a man like him who wouldn't know the bit from the bite and then when he shows, someone will collect a wager whose stakes no one will tell him.

He doesn't think about the small creatures who husband those droppings, who make them disappear, he thinks only about the grass as a curtain. He pushes at the grass until the stars glint, until he has to see that glint as stars and not as armor held up with the sun still on it, the promise of men. Then he stops and the noise of his metal clothes stops, all that banging armor to armor where they're still tied on, stops. He hears the whispers again.

He is tired, tired beyond hearing, tired with the struggle going forward into the grass that stands so thick in front of him, that still towers over him, and the curl of blood on his brow that is still sticky. He sinks to his knees, he rolls on his side, flattening the grass as he rolls. He shuts his eyes and the whispers rise and then cannot be heard, he's so full of one question:

Why didn't they see him fall from his horse?

Accounting for is the same to him as accounting by. He likes numbers with his answers:

1. They had spread out.
2. The wind had come up and whipped away the horse-and-rider's cries
3. which were made late because he did not want to be thought a coward or an imbecile any more than already thought—cries made late from the mouth and muzzle—

4. as the horse was as surprised as he was at the entanglement of the vine and hoof, the going forward and then jerking back, and the going forward again, and had hooked a hoof on the pea vine that likes growing now and then in amongst the thickest of the grasses, the vine throwing out hoops to get more of what sun does come to the roots, and she reared and fell and then he, the man sandwiched in his slabs of metal, fell to the ground which is soft here and gives out no sound

5. but where his hat fit his head he hit, what should have helped keep him from being hurt but so contributed, him falling at such an angle into the hat when the horse took off with her leg so wrong that she tried to walk up the grass, she tried to flee the pain, to heave the pain off, that his head was caught in his hat.

6. He didn't shout. It was unseemly to shout. And he really couldn't. He was out.

7. The horse bore a cross, man-size, and that is what he had been adjusting and falling behind about, that cross, and that is what anybody would have seen, borne above the horse's head if he himself had been in the place of the last man before him and looked back, having heard the surprised horse

8. but the last man coughed

9. and his nearly empty saddlebag jingled with knife and flint

10. and of course the wind howled across his ears

11. and the metal on his body shifted and clanked

12. and then the bugler took up a tune. The bugler was a cheerful boy and not unhappy to be wandering around this new prairie starving, making up tales of man-eating trees and red virgins and sloughs the size of the port they sailed from. The bugler bugled cheerfully and

13. the last man cheered up, dug his spurs into his horse who thrust its own armor forward a little faster just as the horse with the new broken leg fell into the ocean of grass again and again, while he who had hit his head on his hat lay sprawled in the grass, knocked out.

14. By the time that last man looked back, it was late in the day and they had already climbed down into a gully and looking back was down into the roots of the grass and of grass itself—and into the bright slant of the last sun. As far as he knew, the man followed him until they made fires along the stream that cut the gully and he ate his portion too. Then the leader cursed, but not so much to express displeasure at having lost his nephew in his nephew's odyssey of redemption—although he knew he would have to talk long and sadly with his sister to make the loss more tragic—more, he cursed the tragedy of the lost horse. What he followed the cursing with, however, was the announcement of one fewer share of gold, so his men's morale rose instead of sank at his seeming

dismissal of a man's worth versus a horse's. More gold is good for a man. Yet despite such talk and the waning hour, he sent out two scouts. Find the cross at least, he said and omitted mention of the horse altogether.

15. In this dark and the tall grass, they couldn't go far. They circled each other, keeping an eye on the other's hat just barely glimpsed in the last light above the thick waving grass they had ridden through in fear for so many days, and called out to each other over and over until quickly, so quickly, the two hats returned to the smoke uncurling over the gully and the men underneath gave their report of nothing, of a new share to be shared.

Chapter 4

Don't get Me started with dreams. You know when the computer forgets what it's doing and the screen writes in half-Greek? When people dream, they know things like god but the parts they don't know are filled in with that half-Greek stuff. So you have people who come that close every night—or an industry, in the case of fortune-tellers and psychics. I hate letting the god stuff leak out like that but I do have so much of it. I guess it's good that people get some idea of what I'm all about. Freud and wish fulfillment? Dream is more like putting a little beaten egg in the sauce before you add all the rest, to temper the mix, so to speak, to get people used to God. And what do people do? Forget.

They also drink for their dreams. They begin in the afternoon.

On the rocks? Mrs. Hardy peers into the freezer.

Yes, says Bessie. Is it four o'clock already? *Gracias.*

Mrs. Hardy fills glasses with ice and pours while Bessie puts the potatoes on: three Idahos tossed so hard into the oven they bounce off the back. I have to get new glasses, says Bessie. Either I'm too close or too far.

Whenever I see Mr. Hardy's buffalo, I feel the same way. Mostly too close, says Mrs. Hardy. They raise their drinks to each other.

Bessie takes her first sip then reaches into the bottom drawer next to the sink and pulls out cigarettes and matches. The buffalo reminds me, she says. I dreamt last night. My dream is so real I wake up. I feel that way about the buffalo. Too real. She lights both their cigarettes.

I woke up too but not dreaming. Mrs. Hardy inspects the dishtowel over Bessie's arm for holes.

It was very late, says Bessie. Almost morning. In the a.m. anyway.

She draws on her cigarette and looks at the furniture stains across the backs of two of her fingers. A real dream, she says.

Some of my dreams come true, says Mrs. Hardy. You know which ones will when you dream them.

Bessie nods and pushes her glass across the table. Please.

Mrs. Hardy pours in more soda instead of scotch, topping off her own glass too. You didn't dream about your son, did you?

No, says Bessie. That dream is over. My daughter says he is in town, but I don't see him. But I want to see him. Whatever he's doing, I still want to see him. She rubs her fingers with drops from her drink to get off the polish. The dream was in a big field.

I never dream things outside, says Mrs. Hardy. The light is all wrong.

A big field, says Bessie, with birds in it. It is summer, like now. I am walking in the field. There's no corn in it, but something is stalky and tall, very tall, so tall it's over my head, so tall even the sun is less. I am walking but I am following—and being followed.

They finish their cigarettes.

Are those potatoes going to explode? says Mrs. Hardy.

No, says Bessie. She tips off her stool, opens the door to the oven and sticks a fork in each potato. No.

Mrs. Hardy replaces the bottle into a low cupboard.

Bessie holds out her glass. For the dream.

Right, says Mrs. Hardy. She pulls the bottle out again, skips new ice, pours the two whiskeys straight. Then she brings out a pack of cigars she keeps under the rags in the rag drawer. As always, Bessie refuses them then accepts, lighting hers, then Mrs. Hardy's. Thin and black, the cigars fix their smoke under their nails, seeps in under their hair.

I can't see who it is who is following me—many people, I think, says Bessie. I have to watch who is ahead.

Who is that? asks Mrs. Hardy, drawing on her cigar.

A man in a metal hat, says Bessie. It's all I can see. There's smoke everywhere.

A knight? asks Mrs. Hardy. A hard-hat?

Bessie shrugs, disturbing the snakes of smoke that wreathe them both. I walk such a long way I am pregnant. But I am still the size I am now.

You never gained much weight with either of yours, says Mrs. Hardy.

I feel I have the French in me from this man with the metal hat.

I see, says Mrs. Hardy. French again. Don't you mean Spanish? The conquistadors were the only ones in this neighborhood. If they ever were. You know, being Spanish has nothing to do with the color of your skin. Look at me, black Irish—the Moors invaded Ireland just like Spain. French, she says, and shakes her head.

Bessie opens the oven again and looks at the potatoes and resets the timer. There was a lot of smoke in the dream, how can I tell what color of skin? I hear whispers from behind me who say this one with the hat is a god, that I must be pregnant of him. And I have no clothes on.

You and your sex dreams, says Mrs. Hardy. Want some olives?

Remember the time you dreamt I should check the dry cleaners again for my coat?

Mrs. Hardy smiles. And there it was.

My dream didn't say, Dig here in the field, or anything. Bessie picks up a dishrag and rinses out her glass. Just—he is a god.

Blasphemy. The mind releasing what it can't say, says Mrs. Hardy, sucking on the last ice cube.

Face down he was, in water, says Bessie. I'm afraid of water.

I'm home, shouts Mr. Hardy from the front door just after he slams it shut. A chair creaks in the hall when he sits and leans over to pull off his boots.

I'll bet one whole cleaning my dream comes true somehow, says Bessie, opening windows. It was that kind of dream.

All right, says Mrs. Hardy. I'm taking advantage of you,

you know. One cleaning, top to bottom. If I lose, I'll pay double.

I'm not going to swell up or anything. Not at my age, says Bessie. But there will be something to prove it.

Mrs. Hardy quickly shoves the olives into the liquor cabinet. Bessie takes them out again and puts them in the fridge.

By the time Mr. Hardy collects the mail from the front hall table and shuffles into the kitchen on his stockinged feet, Bessie has the oven door open again, fork out, and Mrs. Hardy is at the cupboard, taking down glasses. Quit checking those potatoes, she's saying to Bessie, it's so hot in here I think I'll die.

So that's why the windows are open, says Mr. Hardy. I thought you were smoking cigars again.

No, but we were thinking of having a drink. Mrs. Hardy opens the freezer. On the rocks? she asks. Or with soda?

Chapter 5

They pee around the man with the metal hat so the animals won't get at him—big cats who eat sleeping children, snakes that wound and suck, dogs happy to bite the hand that feeds them if the hand's scent is off—they circle, one behind the other, a bit closer than before, they pee and circle close enough so they can see that he breathes lightly and his beard lifts in the little wind that blows the grass and the smell of pee away.

Let's go back and ask the women what they think, says Tall Pigeon Eye. Let's ask the smart ones, the ones who have not seen these eyes or the metal.

The group groups and regroups.

He could go, one of them says, the way water goes back into the sky, or the way, when you turn your head, birds vanish. Then we will have no god at all.

They should stay here.

Tall Pigeon Eye says how he hates sleeping in the open: the ground is not smooth, there are no children to bring them water, no cover if it rains. And what about women? asks Tall Pigeon Eye. Who will tug off your moccasins between their breasts? Who will tell you what I can't in the night?

They are amazed and silent. They always sleep out during a hunt.

Do you want to sleep next to someone you think might be a god? Wouldn't you rather have a shelter with such a man around? says Tall Pigeon Eye. He is careful not to say this man is a god, just that he might be.

The problem is always a matter of comfort in the end. When people meet god, they want to be as uncomfortable as possible, dragging themselves up thousands of steps on their knees, or hungry. A fine line exists between those who actually enjoy this way of meeting god and those who don't, who simply feel their face to god must be stretched tight in anguish, a release from comfort and the everyday.

They mill, they don't decide.

Tall Pigeon Eye circles them with a stamping foot I like. I'm just trying to keep off false gods, he says.

This is not false, they argue. This is a matter of eye color.

People like to keep what they find.

The camp they make is close to the river the man knows nothing about. Tall Pigeon Eye manages to make them move at least that far away. And this time he doesn't have to talk long. There is something about night and the distance in the dark that they see his point—the problem of rest with something as unsettling as a god in the dark nearby.

Where they move lies not that far from where the smoke

rises from the fire of the others, the ones with horses, but this smoke, by the time it reaches the top of the gully they and their horses huddle in, is air again, isn't enough to see or smell. They themselves sit by dry stick fires so small the bugs attracted by the light live through the smoke to bite again and again. They don't want god to watch.

These men in their metal think everyone in the grass—when they think of them at all—is going to hell straight off, especially since they surprised a heart removal operation farther south that was attributed to a god rather than torture-for-gain, something these men in metal could better understand. If the people had said this is what we do to our enemies, we cut the heart out neat and fling the body down a thousand Aztec steps without mentioning god at all, the men in their metal would have been a little more leery of adding to the spatter. No credit was given for having fattened the victims prior to the heart removal business either—the metalled men tended to starve their POW's and then spatter and leave god out of it entirely.

They believe they have their own god on their side, they have this god leading them to gold. That is god's job for them. It has been god's job before. Why, the century-long march to minarets is barely over, that business of getting even children to drum up commerce by walking thousands of miles through seldom-visited villages all the way out of Christendom to Istanbul and hence to their deaths.

The finding of god in this search includes death and torture too, if the gold is on the wrong side, the side without whoever's god. Though no one's doing electroshock or beer bottles that shatter inside the vaginas yet, this god/gold business has a way of bringing out the inventive in such worship, perhaps the removal of nails or teeth in unfortunate ways that make it all all right, all right for god.

They roast people.

They haul along this huge wooden cross instead of a priest, the priest having shown a surprising squeamishness over the proposed techniques for obtaining decent directions to the gold, to wit, the roasting, and, as a result, he came down with an illness at the first landfall. That is, the ship captain insisted he stay right there with the boat and be sick and rest and not trouble them. The ship captain assured him they would be right back, that just as soon as they finished pillaging and raping and burning and roasting their way to the gold, they would return to ask for his blessing and be off. The priest, perhaps tied down for the moment with some kind of real illness—or some other restraint—did not trouble the captain with further questions.

It is hard to ask those questions.

So he was the one to haul the cross, or rather, his horse hauled it, with him adjusting its tilt to the trot. It was his cross to bear, until he fell.

Chapter 6

Across from Rolf's Big Game Bar and Grill low six hundred head awaiting their fate. Sometimes eight hundred.

Close the door, whines the cashier. Somebody left the door open.

It's the smell of money, says Rolf. You know, says Rolf as he sets down beers for Bessie and her daughter, I ought to stuff a few and give them a good home over by the salad bar.

When you get a chance, Rolf, the cashier repeats. The door.

I've got to give her a raise. Rolf winks at the two women, moves to the door and jiggles it closed against his great bulk. Then he wanders off through the arch two old grizzlies make over the kitchen entry.

Some date, says the daughter.

He owns the whole bar, and all the animals, and all the tourists who come to look at the animals who pay for drinks to look. He gives nothing on credit. Bessie pats her new perm with its own smell. And he's religious.

No, says the daughter.

The cross on his chain? says Bessie.

Machismo, says the daughter. Look, I'm not sure I should be here. You can handle this yourself. She sips her beer as if it is something sweet.

This is how it is. Bessie glares at her. He has had a lot of girls. You could see them stuffed here, alongside the tigers and bears, and there wouldn't be room.

Mom, says her daughter. This is only your second date. And he only called you two hours ago.

Bessie accepts one of her daughter's cigarettes and her lighter. Well, she says, and puffs. He works fast. Look at all those dead animals. You have to move fast to not get eaten by all those animals before you shoot them.

Dios mio, says the daughter. You think he shoots these all by himself?

He's not a liar, says Bessie.

Rolf's not your type, says the daughter. He's Polish, he's *el grande.*

He says he likes my tacos. Bessie smokes, then glares at her again. It's not what you think. I did not cook for him already. He said he tried my tacos at the county cookoff. Besides, he says he will take me to hunt for jaguar.

They don't let you kill them anymore, Mom, says her daughter. He is feeding you lines.

No one else is feeding me. Bessie puts out the cigarette. Look what he gave me when he picked me up. She holds up a ring with a large green stone. He found it with his wand.

Mamacita! Oh, let me see, screeches the daughter. She pulls at her mother's finger until the ring slips off.

It's nothing, says the daughter. Not even glass—it's plastic.

So? says Bessie. I don't have the right glasses, I don't care. The ring is nice of him.

Bessie grabs it back because Rolf's patting the polar bear that leans over her daughter.

You like Maisie? he says. I bought her last week at an auction.

See, says Bessie to her daughter. Did he tell you he shot it himself?

I moved it here myself, he says, flexing a ham of a bicep. Want to come to the movies with me tomorrow night? He winks at Bessie.

Are you really asking her to the movies? asks the daughter.

Ah, she thinks we want to be alone already, he says, slicking back what pale hair he has left. Is that what we want?

Bessie looks down and slides another cigarette out of her daughter's pack. It's a sort of Yes.

I tell you what, you just let me take your mama with me right now. I'll go get a thermos filled, and with my wand, I'll witch the moon up over a cup of coffee. You can come watch.

Thanks, says the daughter. But not tonight.

Delores, says Bessie. Please.

The daughter smiles and shakes her head and finishes her beer in a single gulp. What's with the wand?

I learned to use a wand in Africa, says Rolf. There you don't find just water but more important things, like oil wells. I witnessed a man in Nigeria turn up three masks and a real spouter. Everybody wanted that wand. It was pretty beat up by the time the Chevron crew got there.

He lets the two women out of the booth and then brings out a bough of hardwood from behind the bar. They turn it over.

It looks like what I used to get a beating with, says the daughter.

Your mouth, says Bessie.

While Rolf shouts at the cashier he's paying their tab, the two women find their jackets on hooks at the back of the bar. It's not like I think any hanky-panky's going on, says the daughter, helping her mother with her sleeve. He's just going to break your heart.

I got a big heart, says Bessie.

44

He drives a round-fendered pickup jacked up so high it cruises as loud as a plane that can't get off the ground. He finds mariachi music on the radio and sings to her in what Spanish he knows. *Linda?* he shouts. *Muy linda.*

She puts her hand out to be held. He drives off the highway then, slowing after he turns onto a country road. Stop here?

Bueno. She unfastens her seatbelt and they stare out the star-streaked, buggy windshield at the moon. They talk about the bad weather and the cost of taco shells wholesale and why her daughter doesn't get married.

Do you see your son much? he asks last.

Not so much since he moved to Denver.

So lucky to have those kids, he murmurs, patting her hand.

It wasn't too hard, Bessie says, moving her pocketbook over her lap. Except for the raising. When are we going to do the part with the wand?

Rolf chuckles and heaves himself out of the truck, going around to the back end, to where his equipment's been banging around.

Where are we? she asks, searching for a place to put her foot to break the fall from the high door. The field beyond the truck is tall and wild, wilder than she'd ever seen—maybe it is the dark—the stalks of grain dipping and falling into one another beyond rickrack order.

Somewhere where people aren't too busy driving around, he says, taking the wand out of a fly-fishing case. I've found things here before. Except the tornado the other day sure tore this place up, he says.

He helps her down with his free hand.

She stands beside the truck, watching him position the wand straight out from his large belly. We might need a shovel, he says, as it starts to dip.

That's just you making it move, breathing, she says.

He laughs and it does wobble. Could you grab the shovel? It's around back under some tarp.

She tosses her pocketbook up into the cab and walks to the back to find the shovel. It isn't too big. She hefts it over her shoulder, but its weight hurts the bony part. She throws it to the ground and drags it behind her, down the drainage ditch and up and down rows, following him into the field. I didn't think you really meant it, taking me out tonight, she says.

What? he shouts a few feet ahead. Can't hear you.

She doesn't repeat herself. Her half-decent shoes meet the

45

mud runoff and water drains into their seams until they make noise, foot against sole, the sound of ruin.

Reminds me of Borneo, shouts Rolf. The time the alligator followed us into the forest.

You have to do this at night? She has almost caught up with him.

People don't like seeing you dig on their property. They just don't.

At least the music's good. She's breathless but the mariachis aren't, they blare from the truck, loud still with their chorus of love, love, love, and machismo.

Rolf's wand bobs to the music, then it bobs violently. Hey, lookee here—first thing.

He grins and takes one hand off the wand and pulls her toward him. The wand pitches while he kisses the top of her head. I would do the shoveling, he says between kisses, except for my heart.

But what about running after all those tigers and elephants? She can smell his lime deodorant.

It is a problem, he says, and he touches the neckline of her blouse with one of his wide thumbs, and then he runs that thumb under its edge.

She digs.

The shoes are ruined anyway.

Fifty percent of the treasure is mine after the government's cut, right? she asks, starting to sweat.

He winks and grins. He touches the wand to her bottom.

Exactly how deep do you think it is? she says, five shovelfuls later.

A little more, he says. I think a little more. Maybe over

there too. I think there was a stream here before so the dirt's not so heavy.

Muy heavy enough, she says. She moves around. Everywhere his wand bobs, she digs.

Are we just going to find water? she asks. We've got the coffee in the car.

Water is good to find, he says. It's not an oil well, but it proves the wand works. Not that you don't believe in it, he says, snaking his hand up her shirt while she rests, his wand bobbing like crazy. But there are other things, like I said.

She leans into the shovel and scrapes metal. What's this?

It's something, he says. He bends slightly at the waist.

Just a smashed-up hubcap. She shakes off the dirt.

You could put it up in a garage, he says, and he takes it from her. Junk, he says, inspecting it. More junk. Usually it's a skillet. But I'll let you in on a secret—once I did find a gold Spanish coin buried here. Worth something.

Well, this is half mine, she says.

Rolf balances it on top of his head out of her reach before she can grab it.

As God, I am pleased. Wearing it as a hat is something anyone would do and then wonder why. After all, people will drop a thing, and then motes fall on it and then real dirt blows up and turns into mud and then the mud goes hard and squeezes and flattens what is once round and then turns it into rock—sometimes. Sometimes it's different, things like a helmet get belched up, get run over and tossed back down. I like these chance operations best, they let in air, they keep Me from overplanning and the ah-ha of coincidence in the big story of science that interferes. And here it's Rolf who's interfering, not men in white coats, bright against the moon-light.

She tries to knock it off.

Rolf removes the metal hat and beats it to the mariachi rhythm. They begin to move together. The hat, the moon, the smell of the wet, disturbed soil in her shoes are all oddly familiar. She begins to sing. *La canasta de amor . . .*

He plays bullfighter with a tiptoe and a strut. Using the metal hat in flourish, he goes down on his knees and paws the ground like a bull, his cross dangling, the disk rolling her way.

She catches it and whacks him with the flat of it as he rushes for her. Then he pushes her down and pokes and pries and enters her on her back in a dry spot with all the waving, bending, broken sorghum overhead, the long stalks rubbing.

The hat glitters where it's rolled into the dirt again.

Maybe the wand keeps dipping because of that stream below, far far below, and not from the hat but who's thinking this now? She is talking only Spanish now, and he is not speaking. He has dirt on his face.

Midtune the mariachis stop.

What? Rolf eases himself onto his knees.

Bessie coils to her side, annoyed. She doesn't care if the music goes off, if a door closes.

It's as if the door closes right next to them.

In the name of the Virgin of Kracow, says Rolf. He brushes himself off fast, zips and hooks, then remembers to extend his hand in what he considers gallantry, helping her up when she doesn't want him to, when she is hardly ready.

Does Rolf see a woman with a shotgun sitting in a vehicle beside the truck, a woman with her windows rolled down and the barrel sticking out, some jealous woman who has already seen what the wand can do?

He forces Bessie into a crouch, he crouches.

Rolf, she whispers.

He's feeling along the rows, dragging her forward. He stops.

They listen.

What is it? she asks. What's that? She pulls hard away from him. Is it Spanish? she says. Something else?

Whispers in some language continue not far away—but what words? And two sets—or one? Or ten?

Keep quiet, he says. Keep low.

The words drop into rough breathing, into a cable TV kind of whisper and grunt, a big rush of hot whispers.

They glance at each other. Do they both hear it?

Rolf shakes his head though she has not asked. Then he's on his hands and knees wheezing, moving forward, his lungs pushed somewhere new into the fat of his organs.

The whispers stop—it could have been wind against all the dead crop—but then they hear the other kind, a final chorus of sex between two sets of whispers, and the sound of metal against metal. Or is it?

Rolf crawls forward—leg, arm, leg—and then there's enough light off the stars for her to see his big behind wriggle.

She can't help it: she laughs.

He turns and rears on his haunches, a polar bear with a pale Rolf face. He claps his hand over her mouth. I don't want anybody hurt, he says.

She bites him and he yelps. The whispers stop.

They look around.

The door? says Rolf.

She whispers: It was probably my daughter to see if I remembered my house keys. Maybe it was the keys.

She stands up and marches away.

From My point of view, the direction she takes is so wrong she could spend the rest of the night covering the quarter section, let alone get home. But he's no better, charging after her, then taking off in a huff opposite. If I could have wound them with springs on a track, no quicker could they come back to each other.

So they see themselves again through the tangle of sorghum that's unbending toward the moon, they start and then stop, then they turn and march the other way, over and under more of the plants. Of course they meet again a little farther into the field.

This time at least he laughs. My enchilada, says Rolf.

She has her shoes in her hand and she raises them as if to hit him. He considers their ruined soles and he offers his arm. She hands him the shoes to carry and together they make their way through the higgly-piggly rows until Rolf insists she check first what's ahead.

She's gone, she says, laughing as Rolf minces out onto the road behind her.

You're so suspicious, I'm flattered, he says. Get on in, he says, opening the truck door.

Maybe the radio just went dead by itself. Maybe they heard things, like the door banging, doing things they shouldn't.

Maybe they did them again.

Chapter 7

They post a boy to stand watch in case god goes sleepwalking and wanders outside the circle of pee, in case god wants to take a walk, in case god ghosts around. They let that boy worry about whatever's unsettling, they have their rabbit to kill and eat, their pipes to fill, and their beds to make. Where they post him is well into the grass, behind god where he can't be seen if god wakes and walks.

Why don't they want god to know they are there, that they watch? Men sense that between man and god some veil must remain unlifted, some protection maintained or pretense imposed. A lot like the bra and its strictures, all that double bounty contained, all that mystery and allure made together. Some people believe I'm a-sane, not really reasonable, someone you should think up sacrifice for, keep a distance from, and watch.

The boy watches. The moon comes up and all the metal on

the man takes the moon into it. The boy sees light so dazzling against that hat the man lies inside of that the man is changed into a god for sure. Then no cloud passes over the moon for so long the boy blinks and his eyes water until what he sees becomes a shimmer—more gods, filing out of the metal, metal-hatted and huge.

The boy cries out.

The man starts in his sleep, shrugs awake.

The boy takes a step back into the grass.

The man leaps at the grass in the direction of the boy's step, rips at the razored stalks with hands that come back cut, with the stalks still standing, and no boy.

The boy stays so still a foot away he is as safe as all the rabbits you never see. The grass will keep a man lost—it will—but not a god. The boy senses only a man on the other side of the grass, a man desperate and thrashing. Where are all the gods from the hat? The boy blinks again.

The man gives such a grunt and a crash when he lunges that's all the man hears, nothing of the boy's blink or sudden swallow. Then he listens harder but his breathing's too loud, he hears only his loud heart under it. Nothing else. No movement, no other breathing, no whispers.

He turns back to where he has pressed the grass flat in his sleep. This grass is at least some place, and his, with the shape of himself at his feet. He throws himself down into it again, rolling on his back. He keeps his eyes open against the dark and then, slowly, dreams the dark into his eyes.

The boy dreams too.

Soon the others awaken, and those with bad backs lean backward, kneading their bones, the river beside them hiding the few rocks they haven't slept on. Tall Pigeon Eye sleeps late, despite all his caution and fear while others swallow the river water or spit, then start to whisper about what the boy tells them. They think he's been smoking. Even Tall Pigeon Eye when he yawns himself awake thinks that. They would say anything after a good smoke. But Tall Pigeon Eye just tells them to keep their voices down or he'll hear you.

Those with metal chests and hats and shins lying not so far away beside them, they waken too, but they don't whisper, they huzzah to be out of the grass that is so high, that now curls in tangled brush at the knees of their horses and lets the sky open alongside its edge and the sun shine all over them. They don't mind that the grass thins, at least not this long day marching away from it. The grass took only one man, only one, they say to each other, and not me.

In this same first light, the man they left behind holds a mushroom over two grubs he's found in the grass. He tweezers the grubs off the grass with the mushroom cupped between his fingers and eats all three as a sandwich, bearing down on the morsel with his side teeth, his mouth mincing in disgust but moving long after he's swallowed, with the pleasure of moving.

Then he throws back his head, checking the sun's climb, swallowing the dryness at the back of his throat, and hears whispers that sound closer, sound near him.

The man doesn't look at the sun long, he smoothes his bloomers and pulls his hose straight, reties his wool shirt with his armor around his sore middle so he looks like an amputee or someone who's growing another body, then he starts to march again.

The whisper is a sportscaster's whisper, a golf-match whisper, kept low so the ones who are hitting the ball keep on hitting it, but loud enough so those out of direct line of sight can enjoy the game. Whenever the man stops to scratch his ass or wipe the sweat off his face with his linen, Tall Pigeon Eye, walking backward in front of them all, whispers that they should turn back, that this following is enough, that this is going too far, what about the hunt? The whisperer in front looks up at Tall Pigeon Eye's pigeon eye, and shakes his head. He says, Maybe god will lead us to food, did you ever think of that?

The man walks toward the sun, a direction he knew yesterday. How is he to know the other men in metal have tacked west against a riverbed, that the sun is now hitting their sword sides? He could turn opposite the sun, that is another direction, and head toward the priest and the boat, a route he has at least already covered. But better, he believes, to place oneself in the way of discovery, not to make it hard for those who are missing him to circle back to find him. And surely that horse of his is nursing a sprain but still hobbling, its cross slipping but upright, of a height he can spot.

If he could just see over the grass.

There are whispers all the time.

Stumbling in front, Tall Pigeon Eye shakes the artfully tied feathers he wears at his waist and lets his one good eye stare into the sky as if he is listening to Me. I like the effort, and the wind that is playing on top of the grass dips, moves those feathers. Tall Pigeon Eye points to the way the feathers are dipping and whispers furiously, and those he walks in front of pile up, whispering back.

The man stops to stare into the thinnest grass, stops entirely, watches the grass undulate, listens again, and walks on.

Never mind what he thinks he hears, he must catch up.

But once he hears what? A bugle, or was it a bird from one of the huge flocks that shade him the way the grass won't ever? Was it a bird that made that noise or a bugle?

Even the whisperers stop at that sound.

He stops too, he must stop. He looks as if he is going to consult someone. *Que tal?* he whispers at the tall grass.

When there is no answer, he unbuckles the armor that dangles from his waist, that he makes clank sometimes just to hear it or just to drown out the whispers, and he steps out of that armor, doubles over, and vomits.

To be lost is modern. Man moves from his mother to his woman to his wife and the move is so smooth that the village turns on it, from family to city, with the inevitable logic of a man's place in the world. Women know *lost* better than men, going through birth all alone every time. Only their bodies do the work of birthing, no one else can do it, and they feel lost in themselves doing it. Birth's loneliness gives them this certainty that they have no place, and laying out the dead teaches them again they are lost. For the man with the armor, even the way through that forest he traveled and lost the ship captain's gold is known, known by all, especially by men who hide in its trees, waiting for what gold they know will come and be theirs, at swords-length. To be lost requires a place that is out of this world.

Nausea greets this new state, like many others.

The whisperers whisper from one to another all the way

back to where the boy is still telling about the hat, about the gods that filed from it in the night, that they are only half believing, that they now stop and listen to and wonder.

If this is sickness, is he a man?

Tall Pigeon Eye waves his feathers in the direction of Get out of here.

Kill the man is what they decide.

Chapter 8

All over the Midwest you find people who know I'm here. Why, there was this woman in Minnesota—you read about her in the grocery-line–kind-of-paper who found Me in her dishwasher, on a scratched plastic Goofy cup. And there are others who know there's something going on and so are forever talking aliens. Aliens, and I don't mean just the unregistered citizen-slaves who trim trees and pick fruit, they talk about people of real color, purple, for example, with weeds attached to the person's undersides or insect parts where their mouths should be. Sometimes that same newspaper puts them on the front page with a star's parts. And there are also those who know there's something going on, but they can't quite put their finger to it. What they end up fingering usually isn't God, in general, the human mind always running to evil like it does. But not always. Remember the girl who last year offered her firstborn to the rising river? I was behind her, in my pickup.

Morning, mumbles Rolf from the grill while I'm taking up the rear booth, signaling with two fingers for double eggs. Usually he's hanging over Me, looking down my front for whatever hint of decollete a plaid work shirt from L.L. Bean with darts affords.

Oh, you forgot God's not sexbound? Heads up. Or at least quit staring at that Goofy cup reproduced in color across the front of that grease-stained paper. Did all that mention of broadcasting, of seed getting scattered, make you put Me down as a male? Think of My usual costume, a real sideshow beard and what can only be called a dress, then fast-forward a little, press the amalgam button, add L.L. Bean. Trick or treat! Open your mind the way I open the local rag every morning, the way I read every little bit, which is not a lot in print. I read it even though I know everything, even the truth about the ads to convince people to sell plastic goods through the at-home party method, even about public broadcasting.

But today Rolf's not so interested in Me as in the pager he is nestling into the paw of the moth-eaten Kodiak bear at the grill's end.

Not a minute later, a cop comes through the door for it.

I could have sold it, boasts Rolf, waving his broad white hand from behind the bear. Sold it, and made a fortune. A genuine police unit like that.

The cop clips the pager back onto his belt. That will teach me to get comfortable.

This is a failing of mine, typecasting-by-uniform, but I hate cops. I shouldn't say this but some of them think they're god. I should get my own uniform, that would teach Me. Anyway, whenever I see a cop, I do not like to see him. In response to this one, I waggle My paper like I'm casual and friendly, then his pager goes off.

It does happen.

Doesn't that mean you have to be somewhere else? says Rolf.

The cop turns the squawking down. I'm here to protect you for however long it takes to get a take-out coffee. With milk.

One white, Rolf shouts to a passing waitress.

Rolf likes cops less than I do, but he's Chamber of Commerce, Kiwanis Club, Knights of Columbus. Some of his best friends are cops. This one dates his second cousin.

See—over there! The cop tilts his chin toward Pork, who's sipping at his own coffee in a booth. Pork hasn't changed out of the clothes he drove to town in, silk shirt, shiny pants, and he keeps his sunglasses on indoors. My theory is, says the cop, the louder the clothes the more likely the crime.

You'll be arresting the priest in his vestments next, says Rolf.

Let me just play cop for one minute, says the cop. Okay? Besides, I think I followed that dude not long ago. I think we'll just have ourselves a little conversation. I'm allowed that.

Be my guest. Rolf shakes his head then steps back behind the register to find a toothpick.

The cop sits down right in front of Pork, steels his jaw, and puts his hand on his holster. He's about to open his mouth when Pork says, Excuse me, officer, and scoots out the booth to the door.

Wish I could have a picture of that, says Rolf, watching Pork roar out of the lot.

The problem is, the cop says, taking a sip of Pork's coffee, is that they're all guilty by the time they reach twenty. I don't know exactly what of, but they've done it.

You could have said Stop or I'll shoot, says Rolf, catching the waitress with the coffee-to-go.

Rolf, the cop says. I don't want to leave any holes in your place. The coffee's bad enough. He sips off the lid of his cup.

Rolf barks like a seal when he's really tickled, his arms shaking helplessly like flippers at his sides. He barks now, he goes on like this even after the pneumatic door eases shut behind the cop.

Then he takes a big breath.

He slops a wet rag over to the booth where the boy and then the cop sat, and he slides that rag way across the table as if he means to clean it, though it is as clean as that rag, then he leans way over to look under the table and pulls off a piece of paper stuck there.

I see all this from my vantage in the corner where he has forgotten Me.

Nothing says nothing like something from the oven, hums Rolf, going back over to the register to insert a new toothpick into his mouth. He crumples up the paper. Then he spots Me watching him. He says: Do you need a refill or what?

I look as if I have not seen anything. I do that all the time since I see so much so I have it down. I am not bothered by his *what*, as belligerent as it is, although I do not have the patience with it that I would like. I am worn thin with parity and ranchers with Cadillacs that fart instead of honk. Thank you, I say, and hold out my cup.

A waitress is beckoned.

As soon as I am finished, I drive out to check My field again. Not one of those hired hands turned up yesterday to plow it under, and all that undone growing wears on Me, all that grass-in-abeyance. I follow Pork's route, the one he high-tailed out on the side road to where the goods have got to be, right next to My undone field. The wayward always return to the scene of the crime not for its possible reenactment, or even to revel in the details, but to double-check whether they've left anything. In this case, it's everything.

Of course I know where.

Meanwhile, Rolf tidies up, as is his wont. He crushes My left-behind newspaper into a ball as small as that paper he had already pressed into the overflowing pail below the bar. Then he tells a waitress he will be right back and looks long-ingly at the very large gun mounted over the entry. He bought it at somebody's divorce sale so long ago he couldn't tell you if anybody ever promised it did work. It works there looking good now, as if he has hunted with it and will again.

A witching wand for people is what he really needs—but he begins to drive. Have you seen a black Porsche? is not what he can ask the lady at the drive-in bank window, the only soul available to talk to in this car-driven country. Instead he drives the streets, all the streets in town, which are not many. Arranged in the usual grid, they're bisected first by train tracks and then Interstate cloverleaf almost gothic in embellishment in comparison to the frame houses that front it so dutifully, street after ruined street against its endless concrete. Rolf drives all the way to the edge of town, to the bronze horse put up by the local orthodontist, bolted onto a Boot Hill where exhumed pioneers are found to have turned into rock, a place where he can't do anything else but reverse and drive to the exact opposite end, to the living's cemetery, which he does. This cemetery is bordered by the usual drag strip, providing plots for dragsters about Pork's age and car make, but no Pork now.

Rolf cruises past the one drive-in that stays open all winter offering heaters, and then on to a quonset where half-breeds dance in summer for what few tourists disembark the cloverleaf and need the sight of people who don't really live there either to make themselves feel at home, or at least elsewhere.

No Pork.

Rolf has a moment of enragement. He does not hesitate to stop the car and get out and pound on the hood. A woman dusting the sill of her picture window not far from the dance site, takes the pounding as a signal of the machine frustration that overtakes us all, now and then, since the invention of the cotton gin, and not malice, and she smiles, shaking her head.

I drive by on my route that follows Pork's, lifting My two fingers off the wheel in traditional car greeting. Rolf is getting back inside his car, sulking and thinking. A sure sign he is thinking is that he puts the car in reverse. Reverse is a more determined mode of transportation than forward is. It just is.

Chapter 9

Kill him! is what the whisperers say. The way they say it hisses.

Wiping the vomit from his face with the grass, the man walks on, batting at the hissing in the grass with more of the grass he has ripped off. This hissing might be a snake's, it might be solace. Walking away is all he can do about his being lost and nauseous, with the evidence of his lostness left so sour behind him, so somewhere else. Walking away from the hissing gives him a direction too. He is not lost now.

Ever one to avoid confrontation, even against his own interest, Tall Pigeon Eye says, Don't be too hasty. If he's a man, he might have brothers.

Some of the whisperers make shrewd sounds and nod, and the boy begins again about what he saw in the night: the army of metal-plated men and the moon, about God as light.

Tall Pigeon Eye and the others listen because boys old enough to hunt are men. They look at the boy and each other in the silence after.

Send the boy back to the women, suggests Tall Pigeon Eye. The women can throw sticks to see if he is a god. Tall Pigeon Eye has friends among the women. Women paw at his backside, his pigeony part, as if that will tell them all their secrets. He does encourage it.

It is fair, the others decide, this handing off of responsibility. A god is not someone you take lightly, or sometimes even singly or one-sexedly. A god is not someone you kill quickly, in a hunt. They should ask the women. The women of course would be distracted if they came to see god themselves.

Why doesn't Tall Pigeon Eye just oust the man by changing water to wine or its grass-people equivalent, or stand on top of water and the like? He could do that. But it isn't worth it to him. This man with his metal hat will run out of steam soon enough since surely he is not god, despite all the local stories about blue-eyed mongrels setting up shop. Tall Pigeon Eye just doesn't buy it, even though they have no legends about pigeons that he himself can point to for his own ends. Well, if he wanted to press his point, he could raise a couple of dead, but then he'd have to make appearances, keep regular hours, organize followers—not yet, not yet is what Tall Pigeon Eye decides. Besides, he likes to think of himself as an office incarnate, someone who's around more to do the files and keep the desk clear and the general rah-rah going, and not so much for the personal, as someone to petition and pray to.

On the other hand, is this guy here to help him out? Tall Pigeon Eye squashes that thought, he has his pride, his territory, his people. He has his style. They all do. Buddha, a sit-around kind of god, Shiva, all wild arms and dancing, Jesus, casual, posing with a lot of lumber. They probably had rivals too.

The boy is sent.

He passes the god as he runs from the camp toward the women, but his quiet run is just another breeze and rustle. The man keeps walking. He knows the grass must end. The ocean ended. How long were they on that ocean? Weeks and weeks. The grass must end. It will. He will make it end. By walking.

Unless he's walking in circles.

The boy is still running when he reaches the village clearing. Gasping, he runs up to the women who are at work chewing deerskin. The dogs halt their constant sniff and fight at their feet to greet him. The women give him a sprig of something to help him catch his breath, so he can ask them what the men want to know.

The women spit out the deerskin, consider their answer. They ask him if he is hungry, then they feed him the best they can cook: roast bird, new beans, and mush—no bread since he returns without warning. The best food will test his truth-telling, that's what they know. With smiles and encouraging gestures, they take the food away after he's started eating it, they take it away until he tells the story different three times. If he tells his story wrong, it is less likely invented than questioned or elaborated or toned down.

The women decide what to say, what to do. They don't decide easily, by laughing at the men who are always reporting huge snakes or eagles that lift away their catch as a way to explain why they return with so little. Instead, they believe the boy. It is his first hunt and he is the youngest ever to go—in height only halfway up the grass—and so he is not likely to know the stories that men produce for themselves.

They send the boy to fetch his sister. She is picking beans

on poles they erect to Me, notched poles still so fecund they sometimes root and put out leaves, though sometimes it is from the fish the women put in under the poles that makes them root, and sometimes it is just the way the pole is pushed in. This pole is tall and the girl, hearing her brother, calls out to him to help her, to jump and pick the bean or beans just out of her reach.

She isn't full grown, and she's shorter than he is. You can tell from the size of her feet that her body is reworking its proportions, sending out more growth. This near-ripeness is what the women want. By the power of herbs and sticks, whatever they cobble together out of things elemental—the way they do now with electricity and sand to chips to fix time, to carbon date—they decide she is ready to be ripe. Besides, all the other girls have been taken.

But she loves her brother. He teases her for having only buds for breasts like a man, then teases her breasts. Watch them grow, he says, and they rise.

I see the worship of one body for another. I'm not incensed. They always come back to Me in time, needing something less complicated, more one-sided, less of the body that changes, bodies that present wants no relative can know, and keep on wanting, not being related.

She follows her brother to the camp because he says she must, not because of what the women say, who trick her out in ocher, wrap her ankles in hide, moan and chant about how beautiful she is. She knows why she is chosen and beauty isn't the reason. She is solemn and her face does not give off the glow that beauty does. unless she is with her brother. To be alone with her brother in the grass—yes, she will follow him.

They roll in the grass, alone, laughing silently.

Of men at hunt she knows nothing, and he tells her nothing. These are the men of the village, fathers of girls her age and others, men who complain of dirt in their fish or quarrel over rain and what to do about it. Hunting, these men are changed and anonymous, and show none of the furtiveness they have with women. Even her own father is no one to her, he owes all thought to the grass alone and to the other men but not to the women or children. What would her father say anyway? Good luck, you're doing it for all of us? What do the parents of the virgin ever say?

The men talk of her feet, their large size, and of the swale of her hips. But not of her.

Tall Pigeon Eye is her father. Not exactly, of course, since he is my incarnate. She and her brother were orphans and Tall Pigeon Eye, being somewhat orphaned himself, that is, let down out of a cloud, was given their care, having no other. He doesn't know about the brother and his love for his sister because, like all good fathers, he doesn't want to know. Besides, she is his daughter, she must love him only.

But now custom has it that Tall Pigeon Eye must cut out. Fathers, even in the hunt, in such a situation, cannot be trusted. There's no blame in this. The others would do the same if it were their girl. That's what they say. Even if the results prove what he believes—that the man is not god—they sense, like some high-tech physics experiment, that his presence will queer it.

They don't know about the boy and his interest.

Tall Pigeon Eye exits, stage right as it were, steps quietly into the grass and awaits some arrow or quail call or whistle to bring him back. He wanders and rages, for as much as he feels he's an office incarnate, this is the most important moment of his time on earth, as it is called, and he has to be out of it. Why? Why? It will take years and years of minor miracles and suggestive soothsaying for him to regain his position now.

For once he is tempted to throw thunderbolts.

He doesn't because while he is gliding swiftly and furiously through the grass in debate, he finds the man's lost sword. He pulls it out from between the thick grass roots that seem already to grow over it. He turns it over and over in his hands. Anyone who needs such a weapon must not be god. This is the proof that he needs. He hefts the flat of the sword onto his shoulder. Here they seldom see metal at all or even sharp sticks. Mostly bones. He sights along its hilt to the end, aiming it like the blunderbuss soon to come. He drags it behind him like some kind of ploughshare.

He likes it. He chops into the grass with it. He flings it into the air and it flashes over the grass like a signal. He flings it again. Like a thunderbolt really, he flings it against the wide blue sky under which stands his daughter, already far away, wearing nothing but hide around her ankles in front of the men and her brother, and farther, the man with his head down, plunging through the grass, and even farther, the others with their swords, one of whom spots the faraway glinting.

Chapter 10

What have we here? The Porkster in his Porsche, moping? Sitting around in that car having just escaped both an officer of the law and Rolf in the first degree, and afraid to get out of his vehicle, even to scour the torn-up field he's parked in front of for the drugs, knowing, in that Porsche, he might as well be on a turning pedestal with cheetahs jumping on his hood and a brass band in the background as to expect no one to find him.

At least the car is low to the ground.

No nook or cranny for a hundred miles could hide such a car, and the stretch of land in front of him is as flat as a secretary's ass—what little definition there is is only in those plants, still piled topsy-turvy from the tornado.

He could go park in Jim's tractor barn and hike out to here to make his search. That would be an idea, yes it would, but an idea like that would never cross Pork's frantic, moping, and stalled brain, as he is part of a generation that regards getting out of the car for anything other than elimination, destination.

Besides, he has allergies. Walking through all these fields this time of year fills his head with slough, closes every cavity in his brain, swells his eyes shut, makes his skin crawl. This is not obvious at the beginning, but now that the wet has dried, it builds. Yes, it is not only fear that keeps him out of the field but his AC.

He adjusts its cold. It calms him. He then tunes to the swap shop on the radio in time to hear Evelyn trade her layette for a brand-new full-length satin bride gown and veil which she will wear sometime "real soon." The word "soon" makes him hunker down in his seat as if it will hide him, the ignition twisted, the battery draining, AC full blast, and the problem of the day laying itself out like a female dog on her back needing stroking.

He can't think. He sees the buffalo at a distance, and all he can imagine is all the burgers it could become. He reaches into the backseat for sustenance, out of nervousness and a missed breakfast, and his hand lands on the last of the Maid-Rites he bought by the dozen in the dead of night the night before, after the twister incident forced a delay in dining. Steamed ground meat with a pickle on a bun. Not Mama's tacos in the least but he does not want to go home to Mama as happiness, he believes, will not follow. He has already weighed her seeing his new "Motherfucker" tattoo printed across the back of his neck against the possibility of death from Rolf and found in Rolf's favor, or at least equal.

He waits for Jim to show. Whatever farmers do in amongst plants every day, they do it early.

Myself, I don't like that farmer-dawn hype. I also do not do a lot of machine maintenance that most farmers get into, a lot of choo-choo and weld. They call what I like to do best pasturing but I let even pasture run to seed, getting the county agent out to complain and fine Me for my noxious weeds growing acre on acre and threatening fellow farmers' fallow.

Yet I am driving by as Pork unwraps a Maid-Rite to wedge it whole into his mouth. They're not worth chewing really, not much as food, except for the pickle. But even stuffing it in that way Pork does not live up to his name in style or demeanor, that name laid on him when he was but short and rangy and in need of Maid-Rites if not vegetables, the name given him by his passed-on father pinching his small boy's fat cheeks. Or was it *Porque*? why? in a sad voice? Anyway, he is all lithe body now, a good dancing body is what he's got, and that's important, that's his profession. He keeps the name Pork because his dead dad gave it to him. He didn't get much else from the dead dad. A sister. A year-round tan.

I drive and park some two hundred feet past his shiny black Porsche with the smoked windows. Didn't I mention the windows? The smoking's a nice touch, a further siren call to cops and dealers everywhere. Pork regrets doing them now, their unsubtle demeanor, a point which he considers briefly as he rolls one down and dumps a dozen Maid-Rite wrappers out onto the ground in a way I see he doesn't see Me, an unconscious dump. Does he think about all the fingerprints on his greasy lunch-dinner-breakfast wrappers as they blow up against the severed and bent stalks of the tall, windblown sorghum? Is that why he gets out and tries to catch them? But the first gust drives them off, and then they're blown over toward the buffalo who raises his head as if he expects them.

Pork leans back into the car and cuts the engine. He doesn't look both ways, he just drags himself straight out into the field to get more of the search over with. This is, after all, the point of him staying here and not there, safe, as it were, in Denver.

Rolf has the note, Rolf is cool or not, Pork has to search the field no matter.

He is a long way off from the car when a crop duster comes skimming over the field. Or is it an unmarked police plane? He has been up in a plane that size, compliments of a cousin's cousin, and has heard that police planes are supposed to crazy-eight it if they are actually looking for people—and that they can't tell anything without a satellite anyway. Not really, not that high up can they see him, so he doesn't run or panic or even glance up until the plane swoops a little lower.

He's actually very casual, walking back to his car. Nobody's name incorporated is printed on the side of the plane, it could be anybody's. The plane isn't spraying anything, but it could be looking to spray. Or it could be just looking. Whoever left the bag at the intersection for him in Denver could have a plane. He now remembers hearing on the radio this size plane have these telescope things attached in front and reflectors that spot almost everything. They don't need satellites.

Has Rolf told them about the slight delay in delivery?

While the plane curves to the west, but not very west, Pork bends down and scoops up a handful of mud from the irrigation ditch which he then applies to the side of his unscratched automobile in a clever kind of camouflage, grinding the mud into the finish to make it stick, to make it opaque and not so black-and-glittering–come-to-me-Cleopatra. He does a good job smearing in the mud despite the anguish he feels, losing the finish, but is unable to resist adding a hand print to the side, a sign of coup or the kindergartner's delight.

Human.

Now the car is brown. And ugly. But maybe outstandingly ugly, not the effect he is after.

From where I now survey My fields, those ruined husks I myself ruined with wind and whatnot, from where I wish it would finish in its ruin and I could get someone to plow it under before the season is too far gone and the government handouts handed out, I can see he's now moved from the disaster of his car toward where Rolf convinced Bessie, his very own mother, to dig holes. A good number of holes.

The crop duster has now seen what it needs to and is arcing back in a long, lazy loop to where it's supposed to be. Pilots often get carried away with piloting and add on, that's what Pork decides, changing his mind about peeing into the dirt to make more mud. That's when he identifies the holes at his feet as holes and starts cursing under his breath, certain the bag is gone, is now discovered.

I lose sight of him then—why would I want to see everything when the threat of that is so efficient?—while he inspects the holes with his hands, like a dog. Because there is more than one hole, he is thinking maybe the bag isn't found, that his own digging is still possible. He shows up at the car again, pops his trunk and pulls out all the shovel it affords, the one for snow.

I could say something about the futility of putting this shovel into practice or the desperate measures Pork has sunk to.

I could, but humor interrupts in the form of My guffaws with the sight of him using this awkward shovel's corner to lever wedges out around the holes, and then the corner of it used with his hands on other holes. What he needs to believe is that someone has just taken some of the dirt from the holes to the bucket shop to check as a soil sample, he needs to believe no one has been looking for his bag.

I don't get past My guffaws to warm to pity because Rolf, knowing Pork and Jim get along like thieves, has finally taken off down the highway in the direction of Jim's field and indeed is now driving down this section line's county road, his vehicle dowsing the surrounding countryside with its black fumes because of today's broken or unrepaired something, charging straight on down here at top speed, at least 35 MPH, his rounded fenders shaking like pig jowls over the loose road gravel.

Pork hears him and takes cover in the field.

Rolf dismounts his truck without turning the engine off and circles the Porsche, touching the fresh mud, opening and closing its doors, slamming them the way you're not supposed to with makes that expensive.

I wince, as does Pork.

Then Rolf drives over to Me. Where is the kid who drives this car? Ma'am, he adds, pointing to it.

I take my time, driving up to look at the car like I hadn't even noticed it was parked there, then I get out and walk right over to where it sits and inspect it real close. Needs a wash, I'd say. Maybe it broke down. What do you think?

Rolf touches a still-wet hand print of mud. No, he says.

Most likely broke down. I think you'll probably see him

up ahead, walking along, wanting a ride, I say. I look up at him with one of My smiles that Shakespeare wrote about—come hither?—and he grunts.

He goes to sit in his truck a while. He could break into the Porsche to see if it starts. But not with Me watching.

Pork is holding his breath in that field. Pollen is doing its thing. His nose wriggles, he fidgets. It gets hot.

I have him fall in love with the sorghum cob in front of him. It's no sexy willow branch or something with great bark like Diana had but it puts out its charms. He touches it, stares abstractedly into the sky around it—you've seen people do this, their brains full of something they later can't piece out—and he doesn't move. On some level, yes, it is about sex, Pork does stir, but that's all, just complimentary stirring to show My power over men with mere vegetables.

I myself fidget, check the loose gravel at My feet.

Rolf idles.

Pork breathes loud through his sinuses.

I walk over to Rolf's truck, hoist myself up to driver level and lean down into his window, showing off My not-so-bad wrinkled cleavage that he would suck eggs to grope, and I say: Nothing better to do?

Rolf nods. He is insulted by my comment but confused by the cleavage. He shifts his gears, he puts the truck into first. I hop off. He moves away, though not so fast. He has nowhere else to check, it is defeat from here on out, but he leaves.

Pork sneezes like a piston in combustion, sneezes sixteen times as he rushes out, accidentally whacking at the plants with his snow shovel, loosening up more pollen. He stays low, sneezing and running, until he breaks through the end of the field.

No Rolf.

He looks over at me with suspicion. He eases into his car and even clicks the lock on.

I don't even turn around when he starts it, when he drives in reverse the whole way out of the gravel.

Chapter 11

When she's shoved through the grass, it is as that Botticelli woman, her hair her only cover, which she holds in a curving *s* across her front. She has no lowered eyes though. She stares, pillowed in fluttering background with a breeze that fingers one spot, the grass stiff everywhere else.

Every god deserves a stare.

He has turned to her and is too foreign for her to simply see: eyes, hat, breastplate sticking from his side, beard. Eyes. Blue.

He, in his hunger and surprise, registers her only as food. The ocher over her skin, meant to titillate, looks lickable. He steps over to her.

She sinks to his knees, falls forward to his shins. She catches at his legs, embraces them, and her breasts, those small birds, slide along his front when she staggers upright.

Sliding like that makes him forget the food part, but what else?

Company is not what the lost want. They want only to be elsewhere—back. *Donde?* he asks. *Donde esta?*

She watches his cracked lips move. God's talk.

Où? he asks. His mother is French, just the way Bessie believes, he speaks the language of breasts and buttocks and pursed lips, the language that comes over him in the presence of the female, though he knows that this language is not right. How do they speak here? Only French comes to mind, only *beaucoup de bouquets* and *coeur d'elene.*

She lifts his hand from its place alongside the torn tights, the painful armor, the loose bloomers, and brushes it across her breast.

He feels her heart, its beat.

Dios, he says, and this time I think he means Me. As in, miracle. First it is for the beating heart, that she is human. After his Where am I? wears thin with do nothing, and she increases the weight of his touch and frequency, *Dios* is in response to all those months of man talk on the boat, of sliding between the entrails of fish, of holding himself and others, and of the ship captain's pigs, all of which moves through him, makes him stiff, that miracle.

The whispering stops.

He plunges into the grass.

She follows. He just keeps on walking, she has to disappear into the grass and come out in front of him, to stand in front of him again, to make him stop.

He puts his hand to her himself this time, to see if she is not the Virgin or some apparition sent to tempt him, only to change into wind and its whispers.

She moves closer. He clanks, his bouffant breeches bell.

He makes way.

Has he never had a woman here? He's looted and burned only two villages so far, only brought his sword up and down over a few hundred people. All morning once because no one would say where to go for the gold—it's always the next place that has it and when they get to that next place and the people there say, No, it isn't here, try x, well, he spends the next morning cutting them down (like trees, the skulls tough bark to the heavy swords). And then there is the matter of his watching someone being roasted alive—at both places somebody always insists there is no gold anywhere at all and that somebody does not change his mind even on the spit. This is extreme, this roasting, the man with blue eyes thinks with the priest, but plenty of other people have ideas about where the gold is after the roasting is over, and those ideas lead them straight into this grass.

But at both places, there are women, dead and alive.

The truth is that rape isn't something he can do in public and it isn't as if he's given a private room, a moment alone. When presented with a screaming, hysterical woman ankle-deep in the blood of her relatives, with her home burning in the background and a dozen or so of his companions more or less looking on, well, he is just not inclined. It is unfortunate, he supposes, since he's not going to get a cut in the gold when it turns up, that this is all the spoils he could share but he can't. When he understands that this woman—this girl, really—is alone and interested, that is, unclothed and stroking, he looks into the several directions where the whispers have stopped and even takes a glance above, into the blue, and then he proceeds.

Perhaps she thinks I am a god, he thinks.

This gives him an edge.

He uses a proven technique with those he hasn't courted or considered giving his name to. It is how he cuts expenses, the trip to the orphanage or to women who take the results off to the manor for money. He thinks of his name, his family, his French mother—oh, yes, his mother—and turns her, arranges her.

She, with her so few moments with her brother, knows and fears that god has it wrong. She knows what men must do. She lifts one leg and turns back to him so quickly the join comes complete just as he cries.

She cries too. She is just a girl.

Oh, dear, he thinks. Not to worry, he thinks. He is really only passing through.

By now Tall Pigeon Eye is ten miles away, slicing at the grass with the man's sword, the big, long, shiny sword, and others in armor, although much farther away, do happen to see it glint more than once when he flings it up, and they send one of their own back to see if it is indeed the sword of the missing man and his valuable horse. This man gallops hard to where the big sword is held aloft—what grandeur!—and since Tall Pigeon Eye has developed no agility whatsoever with its long, heavy length, the sword is instantly taken, and he's tossed over the back of the horse and trussed. He isn't forced to walk because the one who is sent to check out the sword does not want to be caught in this tall grass for long. Slave or no slave, he wants to move out of it fast. Whoever or whatever caught the man whose sword this is could catch him.

In the meantime, god rolls off like a man is what the whisperers are repeating. Unless that is a god's way too. They do not notice the wash of dust in the far distance where the horse and rider and Tall Pigeon Eye have come and gone. They are too satisfied in what has been accomplished, themselves upright. The boy too.

God's seed is theirs.

But it is almost human the way the man whines *Donde?* and *Donde?* again, shaking her shoulders.

Where is Tall Pigeon Eye when you need him? is the question they form but do not make though they themselves have sent him off.

The man's *Donde?* becomes a command, not a question.

He won't stop his *Donde?*

She knows by now what he means, that she is less presence to him than absence, she is the wrong place, all wrong, despite what she has done for him and for her and for them. She wipes her face and between her legs with grass, then she runs away.

He runs after her, his metal plates loose around his middle, heavy, bumping the sweet soft bit in front, which still bobs.

Chapter 12

What I need, Pork says in nervous hiatus, is a hunting dog. And not just any hunting dog, but the kind that the cop has. I need a dog to sniff at the holes. Unless it was you who was digging things up out in the field. Was it you?

You're paranoid, says Jim. I have the time to dig up this screwed-up field? I got insurance to file for, acreage to sign off on, this inspector to come. Not even for a bag of dope do I go around digging holes everywhere.

Pork can hardly see above the sandy shelf that makes up the far side of the cave-like blowout wherein lies a disease-stiffened cow which makes the blowout the best place to meet in secret but it stinks. He picks at the shelf and snakes of sand curl at his feet so fast he stops thinking about the stink.

It's dusk.

You sure are relaxed about it, says Pork.

It was money but it is gone is how I look at it. Same as

a crop. Jim shoos off a couple of the black birds that cruise low over the cow corpses really only a few yards away. Pork twitches around to avoid touching anything. So what do you want to talk about? Dogs? says Jim.

Pork holds his smoke in to keep the cow smell out. You won't let them inspect the field for a couple more days? he says in a rush.

Yeah, well. Jim takes the joint from him. I'll see what I can do.

See, if we could just get one of those dogs in. You know the kind of dogs I mean? The ones that are good at finding it at airports and the like?

You think that mongrel that's tied up behind the cop's house is one of those? It doesn't even look mean. Jim throws some of the loose sand at the birds considering the cows, and returns the smoke to Pork.

Yeah, that's the one. I've seen it in his car with him. I've seen it on a leash.

They train those dogs, Pork, says Jim.

Yeah, to kill. I know. But that old dog doesn't look like a killer, it looks like a sniffing kind of dog, one that's good for investigations. In particular, this kind of investigation.

He coughs. This sure is lousy stuff. He hands the roach back.

It's all I got left, says Jim. I dried it myself from what I picked wild down along the Interstate. He smiles foolishly.

Now, listen, says Pork, we'll just chloroform the dog, drive it out to the field, and let 'er rip. We could have the dog back in the cop's yard before the moon is set, this time of year.

They watch a tumbleweed tumble.

Pork takes another toke. But maybe a dog would have trouble in the detection department after a big dose of chloroform. What do you think?

Jim laughs and then stares at the dead cows' stiff legs and the dim light beyond. Look how high the tumbleweeds are getting piled at the far end.

Pork nods.

Another one scoots across the top of the blowout, falls in and locks to the last. Jim skirts the cows to pull one of the weeds from the heap. He lights it and lets it go.

It spins its flames into the wind.

Oh, my god, says Pork. Everybody in six counties will know we're here. It'll start a fire.

Too windy, says Jim with a big smile.

Too windy, you're crazy, says Pork. They look up at the new night sky, at the faint white curlicue of falling ash the tumbleweed leaves. All the fire might reflect on my car, says Pork. I mean, just don't do it again, okay?

Jim takes one last long toke. Looked like a fire wheel of heaven, taking off like that.

What's that?

An Indian thing. Not your Native American. You have to know about religion, all kinds of them, before you settle on one. Jim's voice starts to rise, the way his father's does, talking agronomy. Now you take the Egyptians, or the Druids—

Shit, says Pork, wiggling his fingers for the roach. What am I going to do? I got to do something soon or I'll be as good as a bag lady. Or I'll be in a bag, a done deal.

The ash in the sky is gone.

I'm a done deal too if I don't get this insurance thing settled about all these ruined rows. Jim flicks on his flashlight.

Turn that damn thing off.

Right. Jim fumbles with the switch. It's off.

It's real bad to have lost that bag. Real bad. And you turn that field over to the inspectors and then what? You plow it under?

Jim says, Sure. He turns away from the dead cows. Okay, he says. All right, I'll go with you for the dog.

Goddamn, says Pork. It'll just take a couple of hours. We'll drive your car so nobody will be suspicious.

Suspicious of you, you mean.

Well, yeah. But don't you have some relative or other over in that neighborhood? You got relatives all over town, you're related to every son of a bitch we went to school with.

Aunt Fay.

So how about pretending to visit Aunt Fay? Pork is scrambling to the top of the blowout. Does she still have that long-legged daughter around the house?

Yeah, says Jim, dropping his flashlight as he vaults over. She used to squeal on me whenever I put snot on the tree in the schoolyard.

She could get away with it too, says Pork with appreciation. We'll just pretend we're paying her a visit, that's all. We could even do it tonight. How about it?

Jim retrieves his flashlight and points it all around as if he is checking his feet or the scenery or the battery. Tonight's okay. I might miss some TV, but sure. But I still have to call the inspector tomorrow.

You're going to drive me crazy, says Pork.

The steaks bleed all over the car floor because Pork takes them out of the plastic right away and then leaves all four flat to the vinyl. But neither of them notice, closing the car doors so quietly, taking off on tiptoe down the actual alley.

An actual alley! whispers Pork. What a break.

Jim humps the rope. Shshshsh.

Dogs bark all along where they walk, they rush to their fences and snarl and whine and run in circles and keep on barking after they pass.

Pork's the big problem—he's slinking, crouched almost to the ground. Make like a slug, he tells Jim.

Dogs hate slugs, says Jim. Let's get this over with.

The cop's high gray fence holds back a very big barking dog. Good, says Pork, that's what I remember, a dog of a size, and it sounds smart.

Sounds hungry to me. Where's the meat? asks Jim as he eases the rope off his shoulder.

Pork comes out of his crouch. I knew I forgot something. You stay here.

Wait a minute. What if he sees me? He could arrest me.

For standing in his alley? You're out checking Aunt Fay's garbage for her daughter. You need the rope to haul it.

Okay, okay, says Jim with doubt in the last okay. But don't, like, change your mind or anything.

Pork scuttles his way back to the car. The dogs love his scuttle. Four of them get up on their hind legs to watch and one falls over backward, he's barking so hard. Once Pork barks back and the dogs all shut up, puzzled, but then they're friendly, wagging their tails, barking louder.

He proceeds to cube all but one of the steaks with a fingernail file, the only sharp tool he finds in the glove compartment—a knife being something else they forgot to remember.

Pork makes his way back after what seems to Jim hours later, the steak cubes hitting their mark as Pork runs closer. That's more like it, Jim says when Pork kayos the cop's dog with a chunk in the middle of his howl.

The TVs must be turned up to be louder than the dogs, says Jim.

Go on—you get in there while that dog still remembers who's who, whispers Pork.

It's a big dog, says Jim, peering through the side of the gate. Hey, wait a minute—it's your deal.

You had to remember that, says Pork. He makes a loop in all the rope that Jim has hauled and attaches it to one of the pickets. He tries to pull himself over the fence but it bows and cracks somewhere along its length.

Why not just try the gate? asks Jim. The gate's right here and it's open enough.

Right. Pork unhooks and reels in the rope and reaches over the side of the fence to pull the catch. He then tosses in another steak cube and follows it, tipping over one of the trash cans just inside. Although it's plastic, it's noisy, falling, soup cans tumbling.

It's okay, says Jim through the fence at Pork's crouching figure. Hurry up.

I knew it was okay, says Pork. He stands and Frisbees the last steak whole at the dog. A quick snap and a moan escapes from the dog as it goes down.

What a waste, whispers Jim.

Pork unclips the dog from its clothesline while it's chewing and gulping. The dog checks him out as the-guy-with-the-treats and jumps all over him, wagging his tail, wild to follow him, dragging all his chain behind him.

They run down the alley to the car with the cop's dog following just as they'd planned. All the dogs along the way bark all over again, something they hadn't planned. When they reach the car, Jim and Pork jump in fast—and have to reopen the door when the dog they want paws at the window, left out.

The dog licks the bloody floor mats.

It goes for blood, says Jim.

We're just giving the dog a chance to moonlight, says Pork. We'll be returning it just as soon as it has time to digest its pay. He sticks his hand into the back to pet him. The dog growls but not viciously. Goldie likes rides, says Pork.

So get out and give us a push, says Jim. You know how loud my car is.

Pork pushes it all the way down the alley. Jim coughs it into gear just past Aunt Fay's house. By then all you hear of the other dogs is an occasional yip that sounds like regret.

I am at the window at Aunt Fay's. We have been friends for ages. I have brought over a sheet cake which she eats in small chunks while I perm her hair, the one thing a woman who cans, plants, and weeds can't do for herself. I am leaning over her head with the comb dripping chemical, watching Jim's car ease down the street while Aunt Fay goes on about those bacon flaps they have on the boxes now that let you see a representative slice that is nothing like the rest. I agree, I say. Why, they could be selling you dog parts for all you can tell. Then I button my lip and tuck in her split ends.

Bad breath, says Pork a mile out of town. The dog is leaning into the front seat to pant and lets its mouth juices run
out.

The dog is just sensitive, says Jim.

Jim drives slow, the only speed in his car. He intends to get
a new one, not a Porsche, but something just as shiny, when
he gets a good crop. If he ever gets one. He drives so slow it's
as if he'll never even test drive a new one.

Pork doesn't complain. Pork is onto the subject at hand:
why would anyone go around digging there? And dig all over
the place? I only know one answer: treasure, drugs. Are you
sure it wasn't you making all those holes?

No, Pork. I'll tell you again. No.

The dog curls up in the backseat and sleeps off the meat
until they hit the gravel road, then he's up on all fours, looking for action.

What'd I tell you? says Pork. He loves his work.

Pork leads the dog over to the holes, holding the long
chain up so it doesn't drag. Twice the dog winds the chain a
few turns around Pork's legs so Jim has to yell at the dog from
another direction.

How are you going to get it to sniff what you want? asks
Jim. Now that we got it.

No problem, says Pork, jerking back on the chain. He takes
a roach from his pocket and holds it in front of the dog. The
dog sniffs it all over, then eats it.

Goddamn, says Pork. Have we got ourselves a dope dog.

The dog licks his hands.

Go on, says Pork, go on and get it.

Just then a rabbit shows out of one of the holes and the dog
takes after it, jerking Pork off his feet, dragging him behind.

Don't let go, yells Jim. It's the cop's dog.

Shit, says Pork. Kill the rabbit.

Jim zigzags alongside but he doesn't catch it and it finds another hole. While the dog hangs over that hole, whining and digging, Pork can't speak he is so run out.

Sure must be a lot of people moving drugs if this dog finds any, he says after a while.

That's enough of a good time, says Jim to the dog. Come on. He pulls at the chain.

The dog snarls and snaps at Jim.

Come on, boy, coos Pork. Come on.

The dog digs in, pulls back on the chain with the two of them on the other end.

Why'd you have to give out all that meat at once? asks Jim.

All right, all right, says Pork. Let's let him dig here. It's as good as anywhere.

So dig, says Pork to the dog. Pork gets down on his hands and knees and paws at the ground. The dog whines at him like he is doing it all wrong, then digs. The dirt his hind legs brings up hits a smashed up old hubcap wedged between stalks behind them which rolls to their feet.

Nice work, says Pork, picking it up. He holds the hubcap up to the moon, then Frisbees it into the distance, like the meat he gave to the dog.

I'm home by now, Aunt Fay's hair is all rinsed, the cake wrapped up and the bacon examined. It looks as if they're signaling Me, the hubcap catching the moonlight like Tall Pigeon Eye and his sword, but they're not, they'll never invoke Me unless it's in fury and anyone else who sees a flash from that area in the vicinity of heaven will say that it is the aliens signaling, an everyday irony to Me because I guess I'm the alien. I watch the old helmet Frisbee away, sitting here in my chenille robe—I love all its rows planted down my front—with a cup of hot coffee in my lap, looking out my picture window that, at night, doesn't picture much but Me unless I've got the lights out. Which I do.

When Pork tosses what he thinks is an old hubcap into the distance, the dog naturally takes after it.

This time Pork's not tied on.

The grass closes around the dog.

Oh, dog, shouts Jim. Oh, doggie.

What the hell was its name? Didn't you check the tag? Pork stomps around in the grass.

Reading was your department, says Jim. I drove, remember?

Goldie? yells Pork.

They take turns yelling. After a while Pork throws himself back into the car to stare out at the dark. By the time the dog shows, tail wagging, chain dragging, an old bone I threw out literally an eon ago in his mouth, Jim's asleep in the backseat and the radio's run into static.

Doggone, says Pork, hearing it scratch at the door.

It is so early in the morning on their return run that the neighbor dogs think they are actually dreaming the two men and the dog dragging all that chain and thus do not stir, except to waggle their feet in fake runs. The dog trots alongside the two men until they come to the cop's backyard, then Jim moans like a crazy person until Pork can get the gate undone with the dog wild. Pork finds it awfully hard to clip the chain back onto the clothesline with the dog jumping on him, wanting to play, wanting more meat, wanting anything other than the boredom of that clothesline run.

This time Pork is quick, sure the cop is waking up, about to flick on the lights, chat him up with the Miranda Act. That was one big dog, he says as soon as Jim gets the car going down the block again.

Yeah, yawns Jim, his jaws still tense. Maybe they use him to disarm people. You know, he jumps up on them and they fall over.

Pork's already asleep.

Chapter 13

Discovery's not for Me. I know where everything is: where the emeralds and amethyst pile out from the molten core, where all the little threads of AIDS tease into death skeins, not to mention who's had abortions, who is sleeping with their ex—and it exhausts Me. Oh, for just a little déjà vu. With everything simultaneous, déjà vu is out, déjà vu is not the simple effect of Oh! for Me that people get, that I allow them to get, discovery at its most elemental, the curtain slipped. Oh, I could do it, I suppose. I could do anything.

It is his *Donde?* that leads him to discovery, not her, running into the grass, but Where? the hopeless Where? of the discoverer, fooled into going on. After he slows and she's long disappeared, he shuts out the whisperers who follow, he hears the ship captain's Where? all over again, those roars for his gold, for some explanation other than just "stolen." Very well, shouts the ship captain to him at last but he doesn't mean

Very well but You are a grub and will take half rations for not being killed by those men in the trees, you will stay with those below like a worm and not the son of my sister, and the captain laughs as he is marched toward the hatch, whereupon it opens and he's shoved down inside it, his Where? black and filthy.

The ship captain is no discoverer either. But he's no pirate. The definitions do gray, however. Bounty, not booty—that kind of graying. In fact this ship captain had intended merely to retrace a previous voyage and secure that city of gold—maybe just a river of it—then to hightail it, packing out whatever he could. Not for him a lot of freelance wandering, not at his age. Of course if he came upon some piece of Shangri-La, that would be different, he might deign to discover it and put his name to it. But besides the cash problem his nephew has put him in, he has already lost half the horses to thirst when the ship became becalmed on the crossing and they had to toss them over—in those "horse latitudes." Also because of that problem of cash, the ship captain took a cheap deal at the boatyard and soon the hull stank of its preparation, what looked like proper pitch but after all those months at sea had turned into cottage cheese, forcing him to set anchor and leave the priest behind on some unmarked and unimagined stretch of continent—in short, he has been forced into discovery, a route he had not in the least wanted.

Some feel discovery between their teeth and lean forward off the prow in its search, some stumble into it without so much as tipping their hats or running up a flag, and some would rather not. The man who is lost concurs with the ship captain. All he's ever wanted to discover were undisclosed figures, the gold put back.

What he discovers now is his horse.

His horse is spine-down in the grass, all four legs splayed upright, stiff as chairs in a café-closing. You would think a horse caught in grass like this would just eat its way out and recuperate with a fat belly over broken legs. But a horse with broken legs just staggers on, won't eat or drink until, at last, death stops it. Catching its leg in a second pea vine, the horse went wheeling over until its rump hit down hard and its back broke over the cross it bore. And there the horse suffered until it died, lying in the grass until dead, about as foreign here as a four-legged creature could be without wings.

They circle the horse with the man, concentrically, all whispering stopped, everyone and the man, agog. The long, flat face of the beast is covered with a shield but the rest isn't. Birds have been at it, dogs have run over its swelling, cats have clawed into its hung-out tongue. What's left says it's a god's animal, mostly the size of it, not the shield and its shininess.

Those who whisper stand the tallest in their world, as tall as the big cats stretched out dead and held up. The few trees that rise out of the grass usually stunt in the wind—or else get worshiped. It's worship that this creature calls for. Sure, there's buffalo, big animals they pick off one by one, crawling on their bellies through the grass under wolf skins in case the creatures can see with those bulging eyes, but buffalo charge through their lives as deft as nightmares. With this creature, they sense a tiny prehistoric déjà vu of some animal destroyed long ago, a creature of god's that could be claimed and worshiped as theirs too.

He's overjoyed to find evidence of himself, a sign that shows that what happened did happen, and he is not just something whispered. As for eating the horse, maggots weave the slick flesh in white waves. He retrieves his rope from the saddlebag but he carries no tobacco to cover the smell. Few others he knows have managed tobacco for themselves except for the very rich and those who do the trading, the ship captain, for example, whose cheek pouches are eating themselves out. The man coils the rope until he finds it's still attached to the waterskin, which is also under the horse's flank and no doubt flattened. He coils the rope to that point on the flank and leaves it lying next to the animal because, without a sword or a knife, he cannot cut it. His sword is long gone with Tall Pigeon Eye, but his knife—and the blanket too—is caught under the saddle. Only one end of the blanket can he work free but who would want to sleep next to the putrid flesh it has touched? And certainly not alongside the broken cross. All he really wants from the horse is the horse itself, he wants to be vaulting over the hideous grass into the sky on its back, leaving behind whatever hides in it, those whispers.

All that comes free of the horse is its bit, the man manages to wrench the bit out of the horse's mouth, as well as the wedge of muzzle shield attached to it. He holds the bit and shield over his head and turns to the grass, to the grass on all sides.

They have been whispering again, about the horse. With this shining bit and shield held before him, they go silent.

A lark calls and the sudden quiet seems less so, an answer to the bird.

Those whispers he hears now do not come from the grass, but he does not conjure them, as ghostly a sound as the eucalyptus rubbing in the forest where he traveled with all that soon-to-be-lost treasure of the ship captain's. What he hears is the whoosh of a sword being raised. All those times he raised the sword quick through the air to cut some person in two—that whisper.

It cannot be.

See how he stares at the bit and its shield where the sun strikes it? He's staring at it to see if the sound comes from there. He's not losing his mind, no, not now, not so early on, he's just desperate and confused, trying to find a reason for the whispers, beyond what must be his guilt over whatever he's done to whomever for gold. Gilt and guilt. And if the bit can answer his Where? that would be even better. He wants it to say Where. He's forgotten about the woman, forgotten her leading him to this Where? She's as forgotten as a piece of meat eaten and gone.

The whisperers shift behind the grass, but he is looking at the bit and the shield and the cross and so doesn't notice. He is willing the bit to talk. And when it does not, not even into the wind that rises, he drops it. He stands beside it, gone in the grass, and hears the usual whispers rise, then fade.

He looks up at the sun and wishes he had better armor. The sun takes a cloud over its face, and burns through it.

Slowly, very slowly, he reaches down with one hand over where that softness still bobs, and he pees a cross over the dead horse that lies beside the crushed cross. What else but pee does he have? The shape of the cross is clear. He pauses at the axis. But it could be an x-marks-the-spot instead. He could be just marking—unless he starts moving his lips in prayer—*in nomine patri*. But there is no map and this man is not moving his lips. In addition, he has had so little water—

just what the grass gives with the dew in the sheaves that the tongue can collect at dawn—that it can only be an x-marks-the-spot for Me.

This horse is blessed.

The sun, as it does every day in this season, in this place, takes the wetness nearly as it is offered, so the pee shines but for a second in the grass and on the dead horse and its cross—blasphemed in its splinters, in how it is now only board—and then the sun flashes at the metal bit and its shield and the armor that he hauls onto himself.

Someone groans.

What flashes here but god?

God is rarely where you need him. He has his agenda, his carelessness, his distance. That's what they too think even if they don't say it. So what? Life happens and goes on or we go back to zero, back into the void of the star's eye, and who wants that? So god is there now. More or less. The boy was right, staring into the hat with the moon against it, the gods marching out.

The whisperers nod over the blessing, that's what they choose to do. But they will not soon forget the flashing of the bit and its shield and his hat and the pee in a cross over the huge creature.

Nothing flashes here.

Chapter 14

The three little ships that sailed clear across all that water the first time bore more men than just the big C guy named after Me. The scurvy-faced, pockmarked, shanghaied fellow countrymen who kept the deck dicky slick there and back, bred, mumbling and heaving, wherever they landed, saying nothing of whom they'd bred with before or what spirochetes climbed aboard from whatever new worlds or theirs. Sure, they sailed back, but their offspring, as various and widely spread as the New World it became known as, sailed too. They were, after all, half-breeds who had nowhere to be but on the sea. When such showed up as guano slingers in Hawaii off a boat from Chile and were mistaken for like-skinned mates on a ship bound for Baja, the trip was not without its own déjà vu. Jumping ship in that stretch of the world where another man in armor had tricked a whole civilization into slaughter, they resettled happily in arid valleys where the heat and hot springs matched a region only their cells or spiro-chetes remembered, not having photos or TV to produce the synthetic memory, and there they met the Hispanic a second time, those who, unlike the original, saw the driving of stakes into rock not as something religious or political but agricul-tural. The result of such a confab was lots of jobs for those jumped-ship sorts who were actually more original—even by Old World standards—than those who drank from con-fiscated cups made of a conquered emperor's ears.

This history ends in the present with an old Buick from which Bessie's father set out to pick whatever there was to pick and then moved on because it is the will to move that those in the little ships that sailed clear across all that water the first time gave him to inherit, with no ship but the Buick. It is in this Buick that Bessie is born, but Bessie's mother slams its door shut as soon as she can nurse Bessie and walk at the same time, she makes for the nearest cave, which in this case is the basement of a house covered with plywood and tar, somewhat roomier than a Buick. The father leaves the Buick as a gesture toward child support and bad brakes, and goes on another expedition to pick and move, and it is this car that sits there even now, an ancestral heap parked before the an-cestral home.

I've always wanted to live where I could see out, says Bes-sie. Rolf can even see out from over the bar where he works.

He's not going to marry you, so forget about selling this place, says her daughter. At most he'll move in.

Why get all sad about a place that never even got finished? I mean, my own mother left here when I was nine.

But you didn't. Her daughter reaches for a straight pin. Home Sweet Home. Will Rolf even fit through the door?

Your Mr. Powell is no catch, says Bessie, holding down the pincushion.

Please. She squats to weave the pin into Bessie's hem.

Rolf keeps on asking about Pork, says Bessie. Usually when people think to ask, Pork's in trouble.

When is he not in trouble? Her daughter rummages into a box at her side for a tape measure. I saw Rolf working out. He has a lot of upper body strength.

And how did you see this?

He works out in that room over the bar with a view, right? I have walked past. Upper body, pecs and forearms. I will soon have my certificate to teach classes in working out.

I hope someone will hire you, says Bessie.

The daughter puts one length of hem against another. I don't speak Spanish.

The mother and the daughter do not look at each other in the mirror in front of them. Which do you think should a person be proud of, asks the daughter, the half that is the people who crushed the Indians, or the half that managed to still be alive today, those Indians?

My blue eyes are from the French. Bessie stares out the half window.

Yes, Mother, says the daughter. I didn't get the French.

Don't be as silly about the French as I am, says Bessie, and groans. She can't help it, bending over to dislodge a pin from between linoleums. Lord, she says, *Dios mio.*

Do I put things at such an angle or distance in order to purposely provoke such an exclamation? How else do I get my share of honorable mentions in these days that lack covenant? I have my ways, I am the wind in the blowdryer, the hum in the sewing machine, the woman on the way to the dry cleaners a few blocks away, nodding absently, regally, and godlike in the direction of everyone, if everyone would ever notice.

You'll get the place all to yourself if I go live with Mr. Powell, says the daughter.

You won't, says Bessie.

Her daughter pokes her hem with another pin. Sometimes he lets me pick up things for his wife so we get more time.

All right, all right, says Bessie. So we think the same things. Maybe Rolf could build a mansion on top of this place for all his stuffed animals.

You're going to be late for work, says her daughter. You'll have to use the iron-on hem.

Bessie brushes off the time by lighting a cigarette. Rolf wants something from me I can't figure out. She draws in smoke. I wish Pork would come back for good. That would make me want to keep the place. You saw him getting Maid-Rites?

He has an earring, Mom.

My poor baby. I hope the ear doesn't get infected.

I have a brother who wears an earring and you don't care?

My little Porky! Bessie turns slowly so her daughter can check the hem. At least he's not bringing anybody home pregnant, she says. I appreciate that. And he is holding down a job.

Yeah, says the daughter. What's he doing away from it?

Is this too short? asks Bessie. She looks over her shoulder into the mirror. My legs look good, don't you think?

Your lats could use work.

Gracias, muy bonita. She gives her daughter a kick.

Ah, ze woman of his dreams, says the daughter with an accent that could be French.

I am having dreams, says Bessie. I don't know about having Pork around while I am having them. What does that mean?

Oh, go and buy your lottery tickets, says her daughter, trying to stuff the pincushion back into a drawer.

Give me that. I could never move out of here—look at all the stuff I would have to get rid of.

Mamacita. Her daughter kisses her. You're going to be late for work. Really.

Bessie slips out of the skirt and lies down on the bed. Mrs. Hardy moved me to afternoons this week.

So you can dream some more? The daughter laughs. She ducks through the low archway into the dark room beyond.

Bessie believes she is being reasonable. She believes in the Virgin and the French and how her daughter measures her hem. But what could he be doing with an earring?

Pop stars wear earrings. He must have struck gold.

Chapter 15

They catch her and send her back to him. She must do as he does, walk his way, push at the grass and go. She must do what god does.

This is not very original on their part but, considering the general aim of supplication, it's about the only posture: Simon says. Even her brother is saying it, her brother who tied a belt around her after he caught her and painted two red lines over her nose, holding her tight to him, her brother who gave her his morsel of food, so like skin from being worn against his middle that it gave off his smell when she bit into it, when she turned her face away to eat it the way she is supposed to with her brother, with males she is not supposed to touch.

Simon says, Simon says.

This is more fun than a buffalo drop, this having a god to follow. Let's get everything we can, they whisper, it's not enough to have her carry god's baby, let's have her learn everything a god does so she can teach it. The ladies won't mind if we keep on following and come back with no meat—they've been notified. Besides, they've got their miserable stews to conjure from dried strips, they've got their berries.

The man is not even using his hands anymore to push the grass out of his face, he plunges into the grass the way a horse would, face front, plunges and plunges until his face is cut from slapping the grass. When they push her into his path, he rears and turns away. When he sees her turn too, he turns again to his path, nose first.

Her legs don't step as far or as fast as his, but she's quick because she knows the grass. Those who follow fan out, to watch and goad her—Faster! Faster! But they always stop as soon as he stops to see that she stops or is breathing the way he breathes, and then they tear forward to see them both through the grass doing the same thing, plunging forward.

Straight out from the nose of the horse is where water is, he thinks, and that is where he walks. He walks in the direction that the nose was aimed for, as much as he can remember, that way. He believes the horse had instinct, the way of water.

Water will save him, will quench his thirst, will lead him out.

But the horse fails him again.

A horse in its pain does not go for water. It goes for getting out of its body.

The man runs. Then he walks.

The girl runs and walks.

The whisperers run and walk.

The girl falls to her knees the way he does, feels at her

throat, touches her tongue the way he does. She closes her eyes the way he does. When she raises her arm to pull her hair from her face, they, in the grass, hiss, not whisper, and so she scrabbles at the roots of the tall grass the way he does, hair down, searching for what?

Water is gold when you need it.

He twists to face the grass with its hiss but by then the hiss is in his head if it's anywhere. His head is open with its mouth full of air, snake air, hiss air, the air of defeat, waterless and twisted air. It has the hiss in it. The hat doesn't help. When he turns back quickly, denying the hiss inside his head, the hat hits him on the side of his head.

After that, the hiss is the wind, the hiss fades into the grass's hissing.

He finds a bug and eats it. She chews on air, she swallows. She puts out her hand when a lizard wriggles past him and he misses it so she must. The lizard is lost, must be lost.

Lost. The stars, strewn here and there, don't help him. Why wasn't he a sailor? The moon starts up. He shivers.

She shakes her shoulders the same. How much of what she does makes her like him? Makes her understand how he's lost? She shakes but she does not want to understand.

They hiss. They see the shivers are not the same, one is not a shiver but a shrug, a saying No.

He turns his face toward the hiss, and she turns hers too. This time he turns further, to her, and before she can turn further, he grips her face.

She grips his, a mirror mocking god but accurate, no hissing, and then he lifts her face and head until her feet leave the ground.

A woman held his twins before he left, twins or a full-grown calf, or her death. To say good-bye, she rolled across the bed in her night clothes because clothes for the day would not fit her, she rolled because she could not stand, she could not plant her feet on the floorboards to wish him well, to wish he had not done what he did, to her, or to the uncle with the ship. She was not without her ways. Of course it was his child or children inside. Of course. Unless it was a bull's, he said to her the day of his leaving, so dawnless in rain the light from the candle at her bedside wasn't enough to see her face so with his hands he pulled all of her and her babies toward him and kissed her.

This is not the same. He feels this woman's weight and her warmth and the quick of her breath on his hand and it is not the same, he has lost more with the woman with twins, the woman who screamed at his sudden cruelty, at his having to know just then exactly how much he was leaving, in weight if nothing else. And now he knows the loss in comparison, he is complete with it, as absorbed in it as a ghost in its death, as only a young man can be, in the premature preoccupations of youth in death, impossible death, all the white of his body trembling until he puts her down.

She trembles too.

He lets what he is wearing drop around his ankles.

She has no clothes to take off. She tugs at her skin where he tugs, she touches her paint. She tries to get it all, to get every move right. Taking clothes off when you have no clothes is hard.

After they mirror each other in gesture, thrust against thrust, and the sound of it rises and rises, then sinks into the grass—each animal effort, each quick drawn breath like the last anyone would ever want—he leaves her, he swims back into the tall grass still erect, he swims into the grass as if he would penetrate it, his armor dragging, and leggings, and bloomers, he swims forward into darkness because the sun has set, he swims penis first.

She can't do that, the grass whispers.

She tries, her torso arched. Like a god.

Chapter 16

Nobody bets on sailboats. I do. I have My money on the third one but don't tell anybody. I like to win, it's in My nature and I do, but if I let on, I'll get hounded by guys with computers and methods.

Pork and Jim pin their hopes on Mr. Hardy who's now last but they can't see that because the wind is whipping sand out of the dirt of the beach against Jim's car so bad the windows are black and rolled shut against it, even though it's 92 in the shade and he has no AC.

My bonnie lies over the ocean, Pork is singing, my bonnie lies over the sea.

Will you stop that? says Jim. I already got a headache from trying to watch.

We're buccaneers on the high seas, says Pork. Avast ye, he says as the wind whips. Buccaneers bury their loot. That would have been the smart thing to do. Then dig it up when the coast is clear, when you need to spend it. So now, when I find it, I'll bury it. Anyway I got the shovel right back here.

Pork jabs toward the trunk so fast beer slops down his shirt.

Jim steadies Pork's beer hand. It's my car, remember? And since when do you carry a shovel?

A snow shovel, snow, you idiot. I tried it out already, the corners of it. Works real well. Pork drinks. Pirates have to use whatever they lay their hands on. Human bones, sometimes.

Pork raises his eyebrows.

Skull and crossbones, says Jim. You know, you've got to get out of here. You're losing it.

The wind beats the car.

Where to go, where to go? asks Pork.

Denver would not be smart, says Jim. That would not be smart. Just take the Interstate the other way. That ought to do it.

Jim drains his beer.

More grit smacks the windshield.

Glad you thought up watching this sailboat race, says Pork. I haven't ever seen one, I don't believe. New sport. No one would guess I was here.

Yeah, well. This view is worse than a cable hookup done by the cable company.

Funny. Pork rolls his eyes. You sure the boats are not just all turtled?

Jim rolls his window down.

What are you doing? I don't want to eat this stuff. Pork coughs on the incoming dust.

I'm going to get more beer out of the back. Jim opens his door to the storm and makes a run for it.

Bessie pulls up while Jim's fumbling around with the ice chest in the trunk. Jim, she shouts, have you seen Pork? I heard he was in town.

Not really, says Jim.

Hi, Mom. Pork sticks his head out the open window on Jim's side. Hi.

Bessie pulls her car farther onto the bluff overlooking the lake, gets out and slides in beside him. You rotten child, she says. *Pobrecita.* Your sister says you been eating Maid-Rites.

I would never do that, he says. They're not good for me. Pickles give you wrinkles, right?

I have eaten too many of them, says Bessie, laughing.

Which do you want, Bessie? Jim holds out three beers.

Thank you, Jim. Bessie takes one and Jim moves behind the wheel. I think your dad's boat will win this time. These people from Colorado, they only know how lakes are with mountains around, not lakes that are in the open, like the ocean.

We're pirates, says Pork, opening her beer.

You still have a job? asks Bessie.

I hope so. Pork smiles very brightly. I'm just taking my sick days.

I see, says Bessie.

The wind dies suddenly.

Hey, says Jim, slumping in his seat, if you sight the boats just right, they look like they're sailing on the grass.

Makes me seasick, says Pork.

Your sister told me about the earring, says Bessie. I have a lot of earrings with only one left.

I'm a pirate, says Pork, pulling up his collar so she can't see his tattoo, but I don't think Mr. Hardy's going to win.

The lake turns gold just then—all that dust in the air and the prism of the sun on its way down turns the whole lake gold, into an illustrated broadside for a conquistador if you like that sort of thing—and a big wind huffs across it until only a few of the boats still float.

Oh, well, says Jim, drinking up. Dad's down.

To the buccaneers, says Pork. Me matie, he says to Jim, who belches.

Muy disgusting, says Bessie. I had to come and find you. What have you been doing?

I've lost something very valuable, Mama, says Pork. Jim tries to distract him by trying to take his beer away, but it's useless, beer spills and Pork toasts him. I've lost a lot and I think I'm going to relocate.

Uh-huh, she says.

Wait a minute. I am such a gentleman. Pork dives to the floor, brings up a bag of chips, and offers it to her.

Pork, she screeches. What's that you got written on your neck?

Nothing, Mom. He backs away from her. Nothing, really. Just a tattoo.

She drags him out of the car by his ear. What do you do for work? she yells at him. What do you do that you need a tattoo?

I dance, Mom. I dance in clubs.

She lets go of his ear. Is that all? I thought it was something bad.

The grit swirls around them.

Bad? No. See these beautiful pants? Pork takes a few drunken steps, wiggles the bottom of his loose black silk pants, and falls against the car.

Don't drink so much, she says. Don't be such a party boy. Your father was a party boy. You look too much like him.

Pork eats a lot of dirt watching her drive off, waving like an idiot, then he slides back behind the wheel. Dad broke her heart and died, he tells Jim.

Not recently, says Jim.

Pork sings *La Cucaracha* while examining his bottle and the bird with crossed arrows in its claws labeling its front. Maybe a Mexican eagle got the dope, he says. You know, the ones that swoop down like Moms and take calves, or at least the ones you hear about doing that? He chugs his beer and then breathes. Or maybe the cop got it, saw the bag go out the car window and went after it.

Yeah, says Jim. With his dope-hunting dog.

It's still there, says Pork.

I have to plow it up, says Jim. I get government support and insurance if I plow it up.

I'll give you half the bag—that's a lot more than your share and those handouts combined—if you don't plow it up and we find it.

Jim laughs.

Don't laugh, says Pork. Don't.

What am I supposed to do? asks Jim. It's like asking to find a bucket of sand in this wind. Or a quarter at the bottom of the ocean.

Pirates get rigs that sump out holes and fine screen to sift with. There's already these holes. Pork faces Jim with his beer outstretched.

Unless the pirates are chased away, says Jim.

Chased away, repeats Pork.

Jim sits up in his seat and peers out over the steering wheel. My dad needs me out there to help him. He'd never admit it.

I wish I could see, says Pork. I wish I could damn well see.

Then the sky goes black and the race is called off and I win. My wind wins.

Chapter 17

You think I show you this girl as all girls of this group, as faceless as anybody who goes for group-think or even family in a big way, let alone a tribe, that this girl finds it easy to repeat what the man does because that's what she's done all her life, repeat?

She is an orphan. Few girls in this group are orphans. She does have Tall Pigeon Eye to care for her though he names her something which sounds a little like Charlotte which means motherless so she is always reminded she has no mother. There is also her brother—not all girls love their brothers. Like all brothers, he lives with the men as soon as he is weaned so he is no one she knows until he grows his mother's features, which are hers.

It is just for the mother's touch, feeling her through him. At first.

Her mother died giving birth to her brother. She had

worn her hair up like all the women, but besides the hair, the boy could have been her, alive again. Alive next to her in the grass, touching her—alive in the grass, watching.

He should not be alive at all but dead. That is why he is allowed to hunt. When he was smaller he was chosen to be lifted over the grass from a rope on a pole with a belt around his chest, he and four other boys. They were supposed to fly in circles around a pole wrapped with bound grass, circling the pole up in the air. But to circle that way, a boy has to die: the band around the chest tightens and tightens, the arms fall, and then the boy dangles overhead, blue, dangles and shakes as an offering. What they want is for the boy to fly over the grass and die. This is what they think god wants. All this guessing. You can see the guessing in cathedrals: huge two-headed monsters under which a tiny human holds his breath. Horror or hope, one door or the other. Isn't it enough that everyone ends badly? That is, that everyone ends? I thought that would be threat enough.

To see over the grass, they have to stand on one another's shoulders. Just to see over the grass isn't what they want. What they want to do is to fly and have my view at the moment of sacrifice. Not for them a heart cut out on some tabletop.

Whatever works for them.

The boys believe they give their lives for everyone and they know better than later boys that everyone dies no matter what, and if there's a choice, maybe only valor and honor make dying better. Not easier. Valor and honor are just as hard to come by as the showier virtues.

The night before her brother is to fly, the girl gathers her valor and honor and finds a way to get into where he's sleeping, where she would suffer who knows what harshness if not death if discovered, and she pulls the rope that will bind him to the pole out from under him—he has worn it for a week, for honor—and she chews it, very quietly, very carefully, for hours.

In the morning, they launch the five boys, chosen for their strength and handsomeness, though some want to change that, they want god to bend a little and accept cripples and give the strong handsome ones a break, but the cripples and those not chosen do not want things changed. They are the ones who launch these five big strong boys, who have been fasting for days—why waste the food?—they launch the boys on their poles, they and the crowd chanting in unison so that no one will break down and object to the sacrifice. When sons are sacrificed, it's important that the fathers are there, to show solidarity if not to compete for attention. Tall Pigeon Eye attends. As an incarnate and even as a father, he is not too keen on this type of gesture—it is not as symbolic a sacrifice as I would like, and he knows it.

Nevertheless, the boy goes into full flight with the others, arms extended, lungs filled to bursting because each new breath will make the loops around the chest tighter. At least they don't have to chant too. Around and around the boys spin as the men wag the poles back and forth, the lucky men, uglier and weaker than their brothers and cousins above, men pleased as anything to be other than strong and handsome and brave and thus alive, swaying these poles.

Four breaths later, with two of the boys already blue and writhing, the brother's rope breaks.

It is as if a bird with great wings banks over them. He can't cry out—the band around his chest is too tight—but his face stays fixed in shock or bravery. He lands, chest-first, in the grass.

I have seen this sort of thing done over piazzas of stone, no happy ending there. Here at least the boy has the grass. He is cut from his binding by those who tied it around him. Tall Pigeon Eye says not to—if you're going to make a sacrifice, it is made, let him die, but the others insist he live, their curiosity at his luck overwhelms them.

So much for god.

For months the boy cannot speak, it seems he must save his breath for his lungs and so has none for speech. Then his sister manages to meet him in the grass. After that, he tells everyone all about the land whirling under him and about the vision of flying over the grass for that moment when he was free.

Because he lived and saw what god sees, they let him hunt.

Remember, this small girl is one who will chew rope. And not just for him did she chew it, not just because she needs his love. She wants things her way.

Chapter 18

Was it a dream or a TV special? asks Bessie. Boys tied up with ropes, suspended from a pole like on a carnival ride? It was for the crops, to get water, an offering to a god, I think, that was the reason why they twirled them. I just don't remember. The boys died, I think.

Bessie smokes. The dreams are strong now.

Rolf drops his fork into the middle of his enchilada, his mouth too full to talk. Bessie takes advantage, ladles another splash of salsa over his plate.

I think, he says after he's gulped down enough water, people do a lot for water—and animals. If we were at my place, I'd show you that grizzly in the front room. He came out for water. We waited three days. Now his ear's nicked by so many of the waitresses going by I'm trying to get me another hunt together.

Ay! How can you do that? She sweeps the crumbs of a

crushed taco off the table. I don't see enough serious drinkers in your place. Just the ones who come off the Interstate for TV football. You hunt with your wand, that's cheaper.

Rolf taps a napkin to his wide lips. Bessie, Bessie. Where did you get that name of yours? Was it your mother's?

It was no cow's.

Rolf shakes his head with a laugh, then takes a quesadilla off the plate in front of him. Can I borrow your gun from you, the one you have in the front room? You don't even use it.

My gun? It was my husband's.

Rolf halts his full fork. Your husband has been dead a long time, isn't that true?

Bessie cants her head to the side, the way you would if you were caught flirting. Yes, yes, you can borrow the gun. I was just going to give it to Pork someday. Don't you have your own gun for hunting? What about the one over the door at the bar?

A new thing has to go on the barrel. Rolf waves his hands. Not something you would understand.

She toys at spilled salt crystal. I understand a lot. Do you believe in God? she asks.

I believe in guns, says Rolf. He grabs at his cross around his neck and points it. I'm a sharpshooter, first class. I fought in Tanganyika in the World War, a place in Africa which is what now? I don't know. We shot bottles off the tails of planes for fun. The airplanes would go up and circle. I never did get to kill anybody though, which is good, I guess, which makes it all right.

My daughter says you won't marry me. She says that I am just dreaming, says Bessie. She says it is only the third date, that what happens in a field doesn't count.

Rolf is in the middle of another big bite and his eyes water from the chile. Or something. He starts to flail. She hands him a glass of water, she pounds him on his back. What are you going to do with the gun? she asks after he swallows and gasps.

He swallows again. One of those big cats, he says. I'm going to get the one that got into the feedlot today—didn't you hear about it on the radio?

I heard. The whole time I was wiping down Mrs. Hardy's silver. First they thought it was some escaped creature from outer space.

This place is cuckoo, says Rolf. Probably in Denver you'd lose your job on the radio if you started out by saying the reason for something was outer space.

We might as well be cuckoo—who could imagine cats the size of lions around here? Bessie taps at the tablecloth.

Rolf shakes his head, then he moves two napkins across his broad face all the way to his eyebrows. That was good, he says. Didn't you say something about bed?

I said I was dreaming. Bessie piles two of the empty boat-shaped platters on her arm.

Uh-huh, he says. While she clears, Rolf goes into the front room and takes the gun out of the cabinet. That's just like saying you want to go to bed, to talk about dreaming, he shouts at the kitchen.

I guess that's what it means, says Bessie to herself, ducking through the low archway for the salsa and the napkins.

His reply is the sound of checking the gun works, metal on metal.

Your daughter is so interested in me, he says after she leaves. She asked about my weights.

Bessie's running water, she can't hear him. Eventually Rolf comes around the doorframe, gun in hand, chewing on a toothpick.

How is Pork doing? he asks. You said you saw him.

He has some sick days, says Bessie. But I don't think he's sick.

Yeah, he says. A guy finds some girl or something like that.

Maybe, says Bessie. Want to help? She holds out a spare towel.

He nearly puts his toothpick through his tongue. I don't do dishes. I opened a bar with a restaurant attached instead.

Rolf! Bessie tilts her head back to see in his face if it's true. It's true enough. She brushes past him to blow out the candles, careful that it's her behind that brushes him, not her breasts. Then she flicks on the overhead, touches the salsa stains here and there on the tablecloth, and removes the candlesticks. Well, remind me to open one too.

It's a little bright now for romance, isn't it? Rolf snakes his free arm to her waist as she passes back into the kitchen.

She breaks away from his snaky free arm and faces him. You know what I do for a living? I clean houses. All day, she says. Then I do mine. I think my daughter is right.

How is she right? Rolf backs up to lean the gun against the front door molding.

Maybe you should go, says Bessie.

Go? He blinks, still touching the gun.

Yeah, says Bessie, who sits down on the couch and pulls out another cigarette. You ride up on a white horse and then what? You should just go.

All because of a little dream? he says, coming around to her, touching her shoulder.

That's it, a dream. Bessie pushes the chair he was sitting on back into place with her foot, without getting up. And you can leave the gun when you go. It's a sort of souvenir. You know, it belonged to him.

Right, says Rolf. Whatever you say, my enchilada. But as he waves to her from the door, he swings the gun out behind him.

Bessie doesn't bother to throw his plastic green stone ring at the door after it closes, and she doesn't really cry. Instead she turns on the hot water and starts rinsing. Sometimes, she says to the dirty kitchen, you lose your toaster, sometimes it's the electric blanket. A gun, she says. I just hope to god, she says, and tosses so much salt over her shoulder she hears it hit the floor.

Chapter 19

The girl and the man find the river together.

He stands at the bank, penis out, still waving his hands, and one of his hands brushes against his mouth where his tongue lies, his swollen, dried-out, nearly black tongue. He lifts this tongue off his lip.

Is he sweeping at the water with this new waving he's doing, tongue held in one hand? Or does he want his hand off, free from his body? His tongue fights his hand, leads him to his knees where his face takes over, where he bends, hands thrashing, and lies down and drinks, penis dragging.

She does not thrash. She does not enter the water.

The whisperers sing sharp, they break out of their whispers and hiss and growl.

She—but not he—can see them and their bodies the color of the dun grass, as sinuous and as straight as the grass together, bent and unbent, in the middle of grass. She knows where to look. She hesitates. What does she know about the water that keeps her from it? She senses what?

She is thirsty but she doesn't drink.

Water! exclaims his lapping, his sucking at the stream the way water does to a stone if it cannot go on but must run over. He laps in the thrall of water and then gets in, lies in it with his tongue out, one ear down, half his mouth to the air. His eyes are closed, his body and all its metal clothes tied to it sink to the bottom, his tights float out from him, two eels, and his penis floats.

The sun goes in and out of clouds while he lies there, while she sees the bubbles escape, all of them.

This isn't what should happen now. She knows the lack of bubbles isn't right, that it has to be part of something else, at least part of a signal, but not now. That she knows. She kneels and thrashes, arms up, tongue out. The water, cold from somewhere higher than the grass, hits her head and eye. She forces herself to lie as still as he does, in the cold water.

She knows the noise of her coming into the water will revive him. He doesn't look to see where she lies, he just struggles out, foot by foot, metal clanking, and crouches on the flat bank. He doesn't touch her or her hair that floats toward his boot as he rises, her hair that blackens the river.

She stays in the river where she can't hear the whisperers, their growls and whistles, one of her ears so deep in the water that its noise fills both ears. She doesn't want to repeat what he does anymore, at least repeating this at the river is wrong. She stays in the river until she sneezes. This is all that raises her head from the water.

The man's head raises too. His head has been over a sore

on his foot where the toes join, where some bug has gone on its own treacherous trip. The man stands then, all dressed and wet and ragged, and smiles.

This is the river, he says in his language.

She heaves herself up and the water warps off her, both sides, in a kind of applause he doesn't notice. Then she stands beside him, repeating the sounds that he makes, obedient to the whisperers she hears again, their loud chorus.

This is the river that will not fail him, he says. One way the river is out, the other is in.

She repeats however she can.

He prepares to step back in. I will find the gold myself, he says to her in a firm voice.

The whisperers grow impatient with his new strength. Of course they don't want god dead, but they don't want him to find his way out or to live a long time. That could only lead to god giving orders.

Check the feathers, they say.

Tall Pigeon Eye's job with the feathers has fallen to his son, the boy who flew, who went to the women, who caught his sister, who saw the gods file from the hat. The boy finds two feathers. What will happen is what the feathers reveal when they land.

But who can read them best? Not the boy. Tall Pigeon Eye does not tell the boy everything, he is not supposed to, and he is now very far away, wearing a steel collar and ankle irons even at night, even when he has to go and no one else does, even when someone else on the chain dies and he has to keep on walking, dragging the body along to the next city of gold that he knows is not. I am Tall Pigeon Eye, he says when the men in their metal ask him. He could say he is god and can read feathers but then they will plug him for sure.

Can a god die? An incarnate must. The man with the metal hat shows up, and in minutes—relatively speaking, compared with the waiting—the world is asking for his dying. Who wants to live full time with a god? It is only his coming that they enjoy, another reason Tall Pigeon Eye lays low.

The two feathers the boy drops cross at the base of the grass where even the naked eye can see the lice jumping off. They are lucky: anyone can read what that means.

The way the girl hesitates in front of the water means trouble. They trust the girl to know trouble. What does the water mean? That's what they also need to know. She can hesitate before his grimaces and wild swinging and a penis but not before water when she has not drunk for a day.

They talk weapons.

As soon as men stop looking for the incarnate, they have to look at themselves. A bad job. Think of Cook who found all those islands peopled by feather-caped men who declared him a god, and when he returned to fix a boat they killed him, the knives of twenty believers made enough holes to swamp his not-at-all-god body with blood, all of them stabbing together in the glory of how gods are killed. No, in the end people don't mind killing god. In fact, some say that's why god plays the incarnate game, so they have someone to kill other than one another—though there's plenty of that, after.

The most a god can hope for is to leave a few body parts or shreds of clothing or even just a hat. These few parts are actually more valuable than the whole. People will exhibit a foreskin or carry the shriveled pit of a liver or the tine of his belt buckle, and all they have to do is reveal whatever part they have and they've got an instant fund-raiser, not to mention breast-beater. Actually it's preferable that the parts never come together as a whole—sometimes there are several sets of eyes and more than one foreskin. Pieces turn up. Enough of the true cross has been recovered to rebuild Mount Airy Lodge. Even so, people will worship each little bit and protect and collect more of them. Even the least godlike, rock stars, for example, suffer from this collecting, from girls trying to tear their clothes free or contrive wet cement in their path for their prints or scrape the hotel bathtub for skin. When big stars die—witness the King—it gets worse.

What they want is more than souvenirs. Whatever luck or fame or love a god has should come off with the clothes, with the leftover flesh.

Pity the poor rabbit, his foot.

The rabbit is still to come.

Chapter 20

His father's desk looks as if he upended the files and spread the contents very evenly over the top: agricultural inspection tickets, contour maps, feed and seed calendars and a pile of farm program forms six inches deep.

Jim can hardly see over it. Not that he wants to.

Yeah, Pork dances, says Jim.

Barely recognized him. Hardly any pork left in him at all. Must be on account of his line of work. Dancing. Mr. Hardy wears thick glasses and only now and then can you see his eyes.

Jim can see his eyes now. Over the papers.

You asked. Jim shrugs. He makes a lot of money doing it.

I don't doubt it. Mr. Hardy puts his fingertips together. They are scarred from tools, from irrigation pumps with minds of their own. But a lot of money? he asks. Why does he ask me for money if he makes a lot of money?

Jim shrugs.

His father lifts a form or two. Say, he says, why don't you plow up that section that got hit by the tornado so bad? It's been two weeks since the storm. It seems like a crazy thing to ignore, given the government will pay you to take care of it.

I'll get to it, Jim says. He examines a callus. It's my land, you know.

Mr. Hardy pinches his lips together and fixes his eyes on the section map over Jim's head. This boy Pork—your friend Pork—seems to think I'm just a farmer who knows nothing but cow pies and sitcoms—and maybe sailboats. You tell him—he stops looking at the map and looks at Jim—you tell him, it helps to live your whole life in one place. The cops know you.

Jim wants to beat Pork over the head for the vein pulsing so hard above his dad's right eye. But he doesn't let on. If I see him, I'll tell him, he says.

Mr. Hardy pushes at his glasses. And the cops will soon be on to Pork. They'll see through him like I do—I remember the day he dropped his Pampers in front of my mower. On top of that, I can see through you, too.

Jim's eyes fill up, just like his father's.

You're no thief, that's what I told him. I don't care what of. I'm not giving him money. It's blackmail.

Mr. Hardy reaches into the pile and pulls out a feed bill. It is a gesture of punctuation, a period.

But as soon as Jim straightens his jeans, standing, his dad asks: Does Pork have AIDS?

Not that I know of, says Jim. He likes girls.

It's the earring, says Mr. Hardy. Maybe there's something he isn't telling you.

AIDS, mutters Jim, driving over to the Maid-Rite joint, all lit up so you can't miss Pork's filthy Porsche.

Jim jerks his car into park, rolls down his window and shouts, Pork, am I pissed at you. Why did you try to blackmail my dad?

I found a note on my car, says Pork. I have twenty-four hours left to get the money. I thought it would help if I told him you were involved.

He offers his malted to Jim.

You are on a short leash, says Jim. He cuts the motor of his car. Get on out of here, he shouts into Pork's car window. It's curtains for you, curtains. I don't want to see any more of you around here ever. Go on, get.

Pork sucks at his drink. He nods. I was just checking, he says.

Checking what? yells Jim, waving his long arms practically off.

I guess you don't have the stuff, says Pork. I had to check by doing something desperate. I got a noose around my neck and it's pulling on me tight.

Well, then go on, get out of here. Go on and do your dancing somewhere else. Jim turns his car back on so hard the ignition screeches.

Okay, Pork says. But first I'm going to see my mom. A last meal, you know. A man deserves his last meal, doesn't he?

I heard she's been with that creep Rolf a lot, says Jim, over his revving motor. She might not be home.

That son of a bitch, says Pork. He puts his car in reverse.

Chapter 21

No one has mental health problems in the sixteenth century. It's still pre-Quixote. They torture fools who are usually not, devils who are often saints, and saints who are asking for it. To treat them there are knotted ropes, terrible concoctions of all kinds, and old-time pliers. Now I'm not saying that the man with the metal hat has a problem. He has, however, experienced a few scourges in his time, and once, when he was ten years old, leeches all over his back, though purely medicinal. He certainly suffers no delusions that he's some kind of god, despite what other men in armor have come to believe of themselves and act on. He also doesn't pray, and prayer can reveal a lot of derangement. But the Inquisition is blazing now and not to pray is risky. He should pray and they'd call him sane.

He pulls his pants up instead. He steps forward into the river, in the direction of its flow, with his pants pulled up, his hat on and his armor cinched around his waist. Walking with the flow this time of day keeps the shadows behind him, any shadows that aren't right.

Later he lets his armor bang.

She walks behind him as far as the fish.

She has not eaten for two days. He, three. The mushroom and the snails do not count, they count as chewing, not eating, or as hallucinations. But the fish that now lies on the bank a few steps away he wouldn't recognize as a fish anyway: it looks like shit.

She knows it is fish. Yes, it is rolled in what always survives the trip through the body, and then in grass, and then baked until it is changed, both the fish and what covers it, sealing in the fish essence, that sweetness, and all else. It's a fish in a shit disguise.

He staggers after he passes it and turns around. She sticks her foot out under the water, where they can't see it. He stumbles toward the bank. In her dream of repetition she stumbles too, and they come upon the fish together.

He stops and stares.

Not at the fish. After all, it looks like shit.

This walking and getting nowhere, this always the same high grass on both sides and the river between, is loosening his grip on that momentary vision of him walking toward the gold without all the others. It makes him stare, here and elsewhere. He is still strong in his resolve but he does stare.

Now he lifts his head and there's a cloud of birds swooping low over the deck of the captain's ship, birds that swoop at fish that fly over. He is staring at the birds while all the others club at the fish that now flop on the deck, and he is covering his beard with his hands, keeping those birds from taking his hair, his little hair, which is why they've been attracted to the boat and not the fish. Or they want his beard for their nests, and why the fish fly is for the cockroaches which hide in this beard which attract the fish, the cockroaches being why the men have taken up their clubs and why the ship captain must raise his sword. The ship captain is raising his sword to cut his beard off to get rid of the cockroaches is what he thinks and no matter that the sword cuts a fish in half, it is his beard he is holding, these few wisps that he never had before he had to go offshore, due to the mistake he made regarding the ship captain's gold. He has the beard because he is afraid to let such a sword shave his cheek. To shave like that on the boat would make him shit.

To see such shit is to see what happens if he sees that sword over him.

She stares with him at the fish. When he shakes his hands over the water, she shakes hers too but with the fish in her grasp, so the shell of shit cracks around the fish.

The fish does not smell. Most offerings do. Most offerings have been around. God doesn't pick them all up. While the man flits his hands over the water again, she removes the fish from its case and then the bones of the fish with the same gesture in reverse. When he reaches out over the water, she reaches toward him, another mirror motion, and puts the food in his hand.

He eats as if he is not supposed to.

He is not supposed to. He should starve. The whisperers have seen the feathers, they have their weapons ready, rocks lashed to sticks and razors and bone knives. Who has left this fish?

They do not suspect the boy because he is a boy. They forget that he has not entered the grass the way they have, leaving themselves behind, but has skimmed over it, flown and then landed. That he is the brother of the girl who is starving—that idea doesn't cross their minds either. They have no minds in the grass, they're just hoodlums and hunters, good for triage and cutting flesh from their arms as bait when they're out. They do not think of women at all—except as bait.

Despite the boy and what he wants, the god will eat and not his sister. She crouches behind the man as he washes his hands, as the bones are washed out of his hands, and she moves her mouth the way he moves his, moves it around the air as if it were fish.

All that's left is what coats the fish.

This they leave, they reenter the river, the man with his tights and his armor trailing, the girl watching for the rocks he steps on. They don't look up because of the sun they face, bright now between the curtain of grass. They wade ahead.

He begins to whisper. He moves his mouth around words that cannot be heard, in less than a whisper, as if there's space with no air in it to make the hearing work, like a whisper beyond the ear.

They stop whispering to listen.

It is easy for her to move her lips the way he does. The man and girl move their lips together, standing in the water that rushes up to their shins, colder and colder.

The whisperers lean forward. They are annoyed that they can hear nothing. They are not used to hearing just whispers, mouths being moved. They grow impatient. They have their weapons, their need to use them, their need to show god who's boss.

She can hear this.

She puts his hands where her legs close. She puts his hand over her nipple and touches him.

His mouth stops. He stares into the river again, to where it moves slowly between its corridor of grass, to where it barely keeps the grass apart. What enters that cleft? Not the woman with twins, that woman is not here to enter, that woman who lumbered up to the dock and unmoored herself when his boat cast off, her big belly twirling in the eddy as his boat sailed away.

He is here. She is not.

Reason lightnings through the salts that keep his brain going, including the one which opens up the certainty, the huge vista of certainty that he will never see those eddies again, or the roaches, or his uncle, or those lost bags of gold. It's like that, says the brain. Cleave and cleave.

He smoothes his lips one against the other and bends to the side of this girl's head. He moves his hands over her to where the breast rejoins the chest. He takes a big breath.

He screams.

All the air he has inside of him erupts, deafening the eardrum of her whose breast he cups, his mouth with its smoothed lips so close to her ear. And when he contorts his face with another scream, squeezing his eyes almost shut and pumping blood behind them, she wrenches herself free of his weak grip, and flees.

She runs straight through the grass this time, and though they move quickly to block her, she manages to elude both them and her brother. She is moving away from the sun beyond them all when, in the middle of the next scream, someone at the very edge sights her and runs toward that slight movement of air over the grass.

She squats and holds still.

Prey often head away from the sun, it is a direction that does not have to be thought through, the invitation of the dark.

Hunters know this.

The screamer holds his head and his mouth open but its sound is stopped, his lips lay flat to his face in grimace. The whisperers listen in this silence for the sound of her or the birds changing flight or of discovery, the scream still in their ears while the screamer's tears flow down his cheek and his head jerks.

Some of the men jerk their heads the same because they see it has power: the metal hat flashing in that rhythm, and they are without her to jerk for them.

She shivers.

The hunter pauses.

I see the two heads just strides apart, both very still, a lark swooping over them, curious. The vector of the swoop says Check here to the hunter.

Chapter 22

In a few years, when Jim gets too spooked from the field, he
will borrow a backhoe and turn up the ground one last time,
drive his old truck over to a hole he makes in it with that
backhoe, and lower what's left of Pork's car hood—first into
it, and then lower fifteen other trash cars collected from the
front yards of a hundred miles around into their holes, then
spray paint the whole used lot of them gray, but not until he
has made sure that the angles orient right to the stars, to the
rising and setting sun, to the turn of the earth in its seasons,
just the way they do in that place in Britain. He will have a
book to check these angles. And it is here, in amongst this
collection of cars, most sticking straight up and a few across
the uprights, all in relation to the seasons and the sun, in this
clearing among them, here that he begets his first child, riding upside down inside one of those nose-down gray cars, fins
up and moon struck when it happens. It will happen under a

spray of stars and my star—wouldn't you like to know which one that is?—and hence more radiation comes through the car's tail into the top of the head, the tip of the penis, than usual. The peculiar position of this fornication makes him high, a phrase I take as sacramental, not sacrilegious. I am, after all, on high, and he knows it.

People today will seldom look high, at the sky. They will look at weather if the helicopter reporters make a point of it, they will check out jet fighters and hang gliders going through the blue and wonder aloud why the Johnson's roof has never been fixed, but they won't look at the actual sky. That itself is a sign that no one is looking for Me. Even farmers who have just stuck half a million dollars of borrowed corn into the soil will shake their heads at radio reports but not look beyond their windshields. Even astronomers today look at a chip or a mirror when they look at the sky.

And who looks at the ground? Concrete pourers are the last to look, pouring concrete over the ground for days and weeks and years and everywhere until it runs into a slab with your dates and your name across it. People can't see the writing on the wall or underfoot or in the sky. I often put a little something in the cirrus. As for which star to root for? One did birth them all and that one does hold all against that black Other, which Other is like goblins everywhere, something that simply won't play, that's simply null. So to procreate in this field with the cars arranged just so is to communicate with the star since that is not null but birth, the point of all this.

Today, however, Jim is plowing that field up, row after row of tornado-torn sorghum tall as a man and still bent flat here and there. He has heavy metal on deck and the AC on full blast, and nothing—no whispers, nothing—will blow his plowing concentration. He plants too, at the same time, injecting grain that will show up for the last weeks of sunshine, injecting seed right down deep into the darker soil where the water licks. While he plants and plows, he squints out the cab window, but not because the cab's filled with that special smoke he likes that makes the cab look on fire, that smoke that makes him so happy. Not today. He wants to be alert enough to see if some turn of the ground will reveal more than a rabbit or some wind-ripped empty Safeway baggie. He's squinting and squinting.

But soon it seems, according to the dials, the planter will run empty and he'll have to refill it. The dials don't lie. He leaves the machine and walks to where his pickup's parked, its bed crowded with seed in bags. He drives it over to where he's working, dumps fifteen bags into the hopper and stacks the empties pretty far from the pickup and the planter. There, in the middle of that field, away from his vehicles, away from the tinder of the ruined crop of sorghum, he lights them.

There's no wind.

Remember how much he liked lighting that tumbleweed? Jim does enjoy a fire. When he was little, his daddy taught him to burn seed bags in the field, as an appeasement, I think, to Me, felt for once as god of the field. After all, Mr. Hardy heard those whispers like every other owner of that field before the time of the radio and stereo and cassette and CD and closed cabs with AC. Mr. Hardy knew and does know something about this field including that sound of two people going at it together that Rolf and Bessie heard and that is why he made those fires, why he sold the field to Jim first thing. Jim in his closed cab doesn't hear the whispers in the plowed-up place or the lovemaking though he does keep on burning up bags.

This is not to say that Jim doesn't hear the whispers every time he steps far enough into the grass to chew off a sample stalk and check the crop. He does. But he takes no notice of them because his daddy took no notice, at least not so much as he knows. Why, in a few years he will drive in that back-hoe and paint all those cars gray and arrange them and let the weeds mount and won't bother to fill out papers for the county agent, all because of someone dead before his time, not really because of the whispers out in the field. The idea of what to do about that dead will come upon him in a dream. It will make him think to model the car arrangement after a kind of religious postcard from one of his parents' trips but seen without that chain-link fence that keep tourists off. I saw it in a dream, he will say to his mother—nothing to his father—and she who talked dream for so long with Bessie will actually boycott its flag and Jell-O salad dedication. No more dreams, she will say, especially about that field. But it will be the wild field and even more, the Porsche, that will bring on that dream of the postcard and his field, that Porsche parked as it was on his property in perpetuity since the Buick already occupied the basement house front, and no one wanted it even for junk.

Only setting the bags burning does he hear anything, and that could be just the rustle of grain lost at the bottom of the bags, or the wind—well, there's a little wind now—or the rewind on the tape deck.

The blaze dies down and Jim calls it a morning and drives off to get lunch. On his way he passes the Porsche now parked at the far edge of his field, and no one's inside, no one to curse Jim for plowing and seeding, no one not to say hello to.

Where is Pork?

Jim is pissed to find him anywhere at all and drives on.

Chapter 23

She wails when her brother finds her hiding in the grass, she lets out the thin cry an animal surprised with pain makes, then she goes silent, letting her body say no with its heaviness, letting herself be dragged out by him, leaving a flattened path in the grass at least for a moment.

I like that. Her resistance tones up my story. He could have slung her over his shoulder, wrist over wrist, or broken her ribs with a kick the way they do to women after a quarrel, but her limpness is new and it insists that she be dragged, heavy as the dead that they haul, all that they haul this way.

You've got god already, she says to the whisperers she passes. That's what I have. That's what I'm keeping for you.

She is dropped at their feet.

She looks up at her brother.

He moves his mouth with the others, condemning her in whispers, but she cannot hear his voice so he doesn't say anything. All she hears is the scream. Another scream.

What she sees is that the feathers predict god will kill them, now or later. She sees the weapons and the way they are carried. I have, she says, what god has. Don't kill me too.

You must learn all of god's ways, they whisper. We must know them. They heft their weapons, for her, for him, in fear.

She doesn't look at her brother. She sits up, she stands.

She thrusts out her breasts the way others do in dance or when standing in the sunset where the grass is cleared beside the river and there's vista to see the breasts black against the sky, and she returns to the man with the metal hat because they won't have her, not even her brother who has slipped her another dried sheet of food, and when she stops to stop up her ears with a plant stem, they prevent her, they say she must hear it all.

But he is not screaming now. He is washing his face and hair, his hat off, his hat and his hand scooping at the water.

She scoops with her hand though it's shaking, the water won't stay.

He replaces his hat on his head and wriggles around in his wet tights and pulls at his bloomer set and resettles his armor over his shoulders and under his arms, fussing at it all as if this was why he was sent, this was the reason for finding gold—wardrobe—and he sets out walking in the river, this time going up where before he was going down. He knows which way now.

Or he doesn't, he can't.

The river is mixed up in his head with road, the one that leads him the right way out of the forest, the one with gold still on the horses at the end, but now the river is mixed up with the wrong one, the one he can't repeat and does, the gold way which is never the same and is always.

She has seen what the feathers predict and she follows him.

If only he won't scream.

But he does. Sometimes in the shape of words that die out, in sounds that start and end badly, sometimes in the raw words of no language. He turns and the noise comes at her until she turns too and repeats after him, screaming, willing him to stop, stopping to hear him going on and keeping on.

They quiet, the whisperers. They shake the grass here and there but most of them stay quiet.

He is inhaling for another scream because now there is silence, he can hear nothing but himself and that makes him want to scream, and just then a rabbit comes to drink, a rabbit who wants water so much it will risk another animal in its agony.

He doesn't see the rabbit but she does and she catches it, bent over as she is like a rabbit anyway to avoid his scream, and she turns the rabbit into food in her hands in a second.

He stops screaming while she breaks the neck, while she scrapes the fur across a stone until it rips, while she guts it. His hands move as hers do, as if he has something to do.

She opens the rabbit and unpacks its offal and rinses the insides out. She has the heart in her hand when she remembers she is not repeating, that the spell that joins them is over.

She hears the weapons.

Then the man is crying over the rabbit. It's not that he sees himself in its slick limp form, he sees that he is too weak to strip its flesh from the bone with his teeth. He has no knife, he has no fire. He doesn't consider her and her way with the rabbit, only its flesh and its broken bones.

Why eat god? she says to the grass. This is not the only way to have him.

She says this out loud and not to him.

The wind dies around this. The man fixes his gaze on the rabbit and won't look up. The whispers stop.

He looks up at the grass, he watches it like an animal that is promised something.

Chapter 24

Bessie is on her way to clean Mrs. Hardy's house for free because her time is up on the dream bet, and Mrs. Hardy is one to collect. At the very edge of the horizon that she drives into she notices smoke, and it could be the smoke of her dream so she turns off.

Pork's black car sits on the roadside next to his friend's field. Bessie stops. She gets out, seeing the smoke and the car together.

At this point the wind acts up. I'm not going to say anything, it's just the sort of screwup that does happen. The wind comes up out of nowhere and blows at the dead embers of that bag fire of Jim's that finished ten minutes ago, and its embers start up again, lick at the grass stuck a ways out of the part that's not yet plowed or planted, makes that fire take on a full stand of sorghum that's still just a little wet so the smoke stays low, so there's no blaze—just a little smoke, dream smoke.

Then the wind dies, playing with what there is to play with and changing its mind.

You know Whose mind.

While Bessie shouts, Pork! into the grass, up another side of the field drives Rolf, then Rolf exits from his truck, carrying what could be the wand—it is long and bulky—but is not, and he walks with it into the field, right up to where Pork quivers. There he points what he has at Pork and is pointing it still when he hears Bessie tearing through the grass from the other way.

Pork hears her too. He has already handed over the bag like he's had it all along but that Rolf never asked.

Gun wobbling, Rolf tucks the bag—where can he tuck this brick-heavy bag? his pants are too tight and his pockets too small—he is holding the bag by its neck in his free hand when Bessie, cursing like the dickens, pushes her way into their meeting spot to tell Pork that his car needs a wash bad.

She has to say something.

How does she find her way between the tangle of tall stalks? You can pretty well bet she doesn't think about how to get in, that she just walks in straight, guided by that stray bit of dream smoke and the wind, that handy-dandy wind that pushes up the plants already so wind-pushed anyway, back to this place where when she looks down, it is full of the holes that she herself has dug. The holes she's not so surprised to find, nor Pork, of course, but Rolf, yes, she's surprised to see Rolf standing there with her gun on her boy.

I killed a tiger once, Rolf is saying, swiveling it toward her.

Only once? she says.

And I killed lots of bear. Rolf turns the gun back toward Pork.

I got you, says Pork, backing up a step.

You know, says Bessie, putting her hand on Rolf's arm, the TV's always telling people how to rob banks, blow people away, or chase cars. How do kids ever learn to open a door or talk sweet or get a job?

Both men look at her.

This is not my son, says Bessie, pointing right at him. My son has nothing to do with you, says Bessie.

Pork sneezes. The pollen is getting worse, worse every day. Just leave me and my mom alone, he says.

Rolf hugs the bag to his chest and uses his pointing finger to rip through the two layers of plastic that seal the bag at the top, the other arm busy keeping the gun to Pork's chest. When a white bit sticks to Rolf's fingers, he licks it, then he stops licking and grimaces, then he spits.

Flour wasn't what I paid for, says Rolf.

He grabs Bessie by the arm and tucks her husband's gun under her chin the way they all do when women know too much or a hostage is called for. So where is it?

Dios mio, says Bessie, you think that gun works?

I got bullets in it, says Rolf.

Leave her alone, shouts Pork. He sneezes again. Leave her the fuck alone.

I don't think I should. I think I've been robbed, says Rolf.

Bessie's wriggling against his middle where his member

lies, if she remembers right. If I'm going to die, says Bessie, it's not going to be with this insufferable pantyhose on.

She wriggles out of them against Rolf's member, she peels them off her ankles, holding onto Rolf's arm, the one with the gun. Excuse me, she says to Rolf.

The men watch.

Weird, says Pork. That's my mother.

I beg your pardon? says Bessie. She is still bent over fiddling with the hose but then she straightens up quick and knocks Rolf's gun aside like it is just an accident and lassoes him with the legs of the hose pulled tight in a noose around his neck. Go on, Pork, she shouts.

Rolf is bug-eyed and empurpled—but only for a moment. She and Pork take off into the grass in that moment. Still necklaced with the hose, Rolf fires after them and hits Pork bad, but Pork can still run—at least for a while he's still faster than Rolf, heaving behind with his pantyhose collar and a shotgun and himself.

Rolf stops to loosen the knot, which is caught on his cross. He yanks so hard the cross cuts him, he fumbles and curses and yanks again until the hose tears off and he can breathe.

Fire breathes too. It reaches down and twists itself and comes up around the grass, snapping. It moves and sours the air as it moves, great acrid bursts, a happy hunter in red, breathing, breathing.

Strong from all that hole digging and housekeeping, Bessie pulls the hit Pork onto her back, fireman-style, when he falters. It is not the way she dreamt of carrying a child, but she carries him anyway, low, his head next to hers, she carries him as fast as she can away from Rolf. Then she lowers him, holds his head to her breast and moans, seeing his blood.

Rolf hears the moans, or one of them.

While he's swiveling his head, the fire goes off instead of his gun, not two feet away, two easy blood-marked feet, a boom and a crackle, and he whips away from the moans with the gun up in time to see two rabbits leap in front of it. He shoots automatically, a hunter's hunter.

The rabbits soar away, soar as if they've finally remembered what to do, standing around blinking in the sunlight for all those years, all those generations, as if the stewardess of the land—not just on planes, oh no—opened the doors marked exit and inflated the slide.

The rabbits don't die.

It's not too digressive to mention the crop duster that is now flying over again, the one that buzzed Pork for fun because no one else was there to be buzzed, who caused him to ruin his car with mud, and is now filled with what fascination people have with fire, and the confusions that arise when anything unusual happens, especially big fires seen from above, that crop duster swoops low with its blades turning, two big fans, to have a good look—whereupon the fire inflates the field, a red balloon swelling fast.

Bessie drags Pork out of the grass to where Jim has left just dirt and stubble for acres but Rolf doesn't follow. He is lost. He can't find his way around in the sudden conflagration, out of the grass that still sways so high here and there over his head, out of the smoke that swirls in and out of the grass that sways, out of the fire that the wind sways out over the irrigation ditch and beyond, far beyond. The fire is what he runs into because that's where he's going, because he can't go anywhere else.

Already you can hear the volunteers and their vehicles in approach. The pilot of the plane has called them on his radio, surprised by remorse. Fearing that they will figure out the size of the fire is all his fault, he doesn't say he's close, he says he's three sections away, that there's a lot of smoke.

Where the volunteers park—in a corner that Jim has not yet plowed—a light snow has spread. The bag of white is open, a bag no one, least of all Pork, has seen. The volunteers grind its white into the dirt as they run back and forth to the truck in the middle of the field, until there is nothing white to speak of under their feet.

To find the bag now is too coincidental? All the time there's coincidence, chaos theory writ large and larger, but I don't let you see it, though the patterns might amuse you the way Eat At Rolf's in cloud clusters across the sky from a plane always gets a smile. Of course the bag is still in the field—nobody's found it. Of course that's where the volunteers drive to, of course it's in a corner—a corner in a field is not always where right angles meet along a highway, the first place you look, but somewhere inconspicuous, opposite where Jim ran out of seed, and besides, the bag was as covered with mud as Pork's car. Except for what gets tracked out, you'd never notice there is anything white to it. The volunteers don't notice it at all because they're otherwise excited, shouting at some neighbor who comes running over.

Myself.

Much deeper into the field, wind from the hot and cold breaths of the fire fights around Rolf, who can't figure out which way to turn in the windy smoke and who trips on one of the pea vines still infesting the field and his gun fires again and this time it's at himself, aimed accidentally. Like a horse in pain, he cantilevers himself upright again, but does not go forward, he meets the ground with a blown-open cheek.

Chapter 25

He watches the flies feed on the rabbit without its skin. He tells her in his language how the rabbit is too small for his people, so small children would use it to play at roasting. They would get a coal from the hearth and turn the rabbit on sticks—*boucan*—over green kindling in a cave. Then the children would eat the rabbit when no one was watching.

She says they will eat it raw.

He shakes his head back and forth as if he understands but doesn't agree with her. His armor clanks with him as he shakes, he is that vigorous in disagreement. Knee-deep in water, he clanks in the face of the sun as it wanes.

He wants to roast that rabbit. He thinks of the children again, the turning spit in the dark cave they've hollowed for themselves. How did they make that kindling light?

He takes off his hat and angles it so the last sun hits inside it where a dent from his fall takes in all its brightness.

The last rays hit the hat hard, the last rays being especially bright because the coming darkness is in contrast, and what light there is jumps when it hits that tin hat and then hits elsewhere, hits the grass, the hot dry tall grass.

There is a little wind involved.

He is not thinking about what might happen to all the grass with this light off his hat, the raw rabbit is all that's in his head. His thinking is separate now from what's around him because of his lack of food, because he is being swallowed by the ocean of grass, rustling and whispering, with nothing to swallow. He has only one other thought: to be in the woods with the gold on the horses, the boat still in the harbor and a hat just like this one in his hand so he can see, reflected, those up in the trees.

She holds the rabbit in her hands, gray and slick without its skin, and faces the sun too. The chill of the night lies right behind its light and that chill travels along her skin, which is against the flesh of the rabbit quivering in death. She hasn't quite figured out what to do with the rabbit, where to find fire.

The grass goes white with the sun.

Then red. Smoke rims it, writhes from the grass at the end of the light that he holds against his hat.

I've always liked offerings of incense of any kind. Out of all the foolish sacrifices: sons, first grain, fermented fruit, thrown coins covering half a pool, honey rubbed on charcoal—I like smoke best. It gives Me cover, it lets Me sneak out and enjoy myself. That anyone should give up what is most precious in obeisance to Me remains a frequently held but laughable belief. Gifts to god! You may as well try to find one your mother likes. What can God need? God takes and slips away.

The fire spreads quickly and actual flames surprise the man out of his stare. While she coaxes those flames up, a few escape. These flames jump and cross the creek and work the length of the riverbank and back, quickly. The man jumps too, out of the water, and then back in, and the roar of the flames that follow covers the whispers finally.

She throws the rabbit at the fire—as an offering? or as a measure of her hunger, still hoping it will cook?—then she jumps into the water too. The rabbit sizzles and cooks and burns in a sudden whoosh of brush fire. Beyond it, whisperers burn or run or jump into the river while she submerges herself, while the sun sets on the color of flame.

The man squats, then lies down in the river, letting the river protect him, keeping just his nose above the water in the ash and heat. She lies down beside him just the way he has, as if she has learned his ways, as if this were a bed of grass and not a river that they soak their ears and eyes in, and she goes under too, her lids parched, her lips seared, her eyes hardly in their sockets, the blood surging so far away. They lie together.

At least the water warms up.

He makes the fire but he can't keep it.

I guess that is the proof, if only those who whispered could see it.

The day seems much longer so bright with all that fire, the grass being so light and dry that it blazes for a long time, gets generous with itself, with its long sweeping flames that flare over grass taller than a man to another tall part where no man can be seen, where men run with the rabbits, or where men who watch and whisper, get trapped and die.

Chapter 26

A basement house is not for the claustrophobic. When Pork sits up two days later, it is to get out. Bessie's in the kitchen looking for a water glass and doesn't see him lean forward on his elbows and check for his shoes.

That buffalo used to watch me, she's saying to his sister at the sink, that big brown head would turn itself sideways in the field to take me in every time I drove by. That buffalo had eyes the size of dinner plates. I didn't dream him because he is too real. Not like Pork's dream.

That was too real, says his sister. She has a tear, a real tear for her brother, and he sees it as she passes his room with a basket of laundry.

Go on to your Mr. Powell now, says Bessie after her. Aren't you late?

At two, she says. Not yet. The sitter is there.

Bessie walks in and sees him blinking. Are you cold? What are you doing with your shoes on, my *chorizo*.

He is even thinner than before and his skin is almost transparent around his bandages. He is wearing her silk kimono from Okinawa that a drunk gave her for kissing him. That's all she ever said about it.

You're awake, says his sister, coming past his door again with folded shirts.

You had a lot of drugs, says Bessie.

Drugs, says his sister, snorting.

How are you feeling? asks Bessie.

He wiggles his toes.

At the scene of the accident nobody rushed up to help you, his sister says, stopped at the door. Not after getting blood all over. It was the earring.

What about the earring? says Pork, feeling for it.

You have the prettiest blue eyes, says his mother. She takes his hand.

You don't know? You can't guess? asks his sister.

Mr. Hardy had to come in and save you, says Bessie. He stopped the blood with his belt. He took it off and wrapped it around the bloody part, what they call a "flesh wound" now. The volunteers were all still pouring alcohol on their gloves while you were bleeding everywhere.

It was the tattoo really, says the daughter. And the earring.

All the fire going on and raging and the department driving this way and that and you with a gunshot wound from your father's own gun, the smoke everywhere and me screaming because you were bleeding all over and I was still afraid of Rolf. Bessie makes him drink from her glass of water.

His sister laughs. What a mess. Good thing you fainted.

Mom, you weren't afraid of Rolf, says Pork.

I killed him, didn't I? says Bessie. With my hose. Best pair of $.99 hose I ever did buy. Poor Rolf.

Sort of, says her daughter. She is looking for her cigarettes. Hey—did you see? Jim's neighbor left a big ham. She points to an aluminum mound taking up most of a table on the way to the kitchen.

A whole ham? asks Bessie. I never said three words to that woman in my entire life.

She's not so bad, says Pork. She helped me once when I was hiding from Rolf.

Take this medicine. Bessie pulls a container from her pocket. With the rest of the water.

He takes two and drains the glass. Where's Jim now?

He's putting the buffalo away. It will take three men and a tractor to drag it over to the blowout.

Mrs. Hardy says it died of strangulation from a piece of Styrofoam, says his sister. One of the Big Mac boxes somebody off the Interstate tried to feed to it whole.

I don't think that was it, says Pork. They're pretty tough. It could've been something else. He shrugs off the kimono. I've got to talk to Jim.

You just lay back, says Bessie. Try this bit of a burrito your sister just slapped together.

He glares at Bessie, but when his sister returns with the plastic-wrapped bundle, he peels it and chews it and looks out on the casement's ankle-deep piece of vista, vista that shows only the Buick's right front tire. But surely his Porsche is out there too, and out there is where he will go, his beautiful car splendid in washed recovery, his suede-shod dancing feet as fast as ever, faster than the dark that will fall long after he drives away, opposite in direction from Denver.

But first Bessie must do her talking. He won't be involved with drugs anymore, he really won't, because Bessie has seen it in a dream, just last night's. No, he will break his ankle, she tells him, and he will have to retire from dancing and with his unemployment checks he will move to San Diego where he will find a place for her and his sister and they will sell hot dogs from a pier only on Saturdays and Sundays.

She does dream.

He drives over to Mr. Hardy's on his way out of town. He's got something to say to him, something like not to worry and thanks. And he has to give the belt back which is the only reason Bessie let him out of her sight to start with.

Mrs. Hardy is fooling with the flowers around in front so he stalls, he doesn't park and say, Mrs. Hardy, I'm here, and bother her. She's a little hard of hearing anyway, especially this time of day when she's so tipsy. Then she goes in, and he's barely eased out of the car with both feet on the pavement when Jim drives up, jumps out of his car and comes at him with his fists clenched. What do you want now?

Pork is no dummy. He could say what he needs to about not having AIDS but not now. To avoid a black eye or worse, he gets right back into his car and he floors it.

It's a car chase. They drive through stop signs all the way to the cemetery, they drive out past the feedlot, past Jim's field, all the way to where the Interstate is under new construction. Pork has him now, he knows on the straight he can beat him easy, he can drive all the way into the dark like one of those racecar drivers with a motor the same as the one on this Porsche, and Jim can't touch him, Jim will be eating his dust, Jim will be packing popcorn.

Pork pours on the speed. At last.

There's just this overpass out of town, with its barricades. They've always got these damn barricades up so that nobody can drive by to see the construction workers not working. Well, damn them. Pork leans into the curve then shifts down, four, three, two—swerves between those barricades as easy as melted butter, then floors it again.

Jim stops short, a fender short of plowing through the first one. What is Pork thinking? He is not quite out of the car when he hears the crash.

Pork has driven off the end of the overpass, where the road runs out all at once, where it hangs, ten feet up in the air, from where Pork has fallen.

The Porsche's front end is toast.

It is while Jim is using the backhoe to dig the hole to bury the ruined Porsche in its final resting place in the field of the other uprighted wrecks that he has gathered to commemorate his friend that he uncovers the cross. Another inch deeper with the backhoe and he would've gouged it to splinters. He moves the machine and digs at another spot a foot farther—and finds another two feet of it. An old railroad tie is what he thinks it is first. Or a stray fence post. But it looks way too old. He backs up the backhoe and tries another hole, like maybe while he's not watching the wood will just sink back into the dirt, then he exits the cab and stands looking into the new hole.

There's a crosspiece.

It's a sign from Pork is what he decides, as indeed it is, as the man with the hat was Pork's dad's dad's dad's dad's dad's dad, though Jim has no way of knowing that. In Pork's honor he shifts the Porsche a foot to the left of the cross and leaves it there. He tells anyone who notices that the cars are planted in exactly the same configuration as the stones in England only the earth bells at this part, it's the shape of the land, what can you do?

There's a ridge over it today where sunflowers bloom especially happy.

Chapter 27

Dawn of day six in a god's life and his last: urine slides down his leg as he staggers across the cinders, as he sees the countryside, flat in all directions, open at last, its curtain of grass ripped down to a sky full of cinders.

All the rest is black.

And silent.

Like the hole into which even I will eventually implode, I might add, on its turn to turn itself inside out, the forever reversible and ever reserved. Like they say in that country with the many-armed gods, I am conundrum. Which is like fire, consuming and consumed.

They have their sun that dawn, the same one that caught on his hat, then the grass. Black runs to the edges of this sun and there it pulses.

The girl behind him bends to the riverbank and touches a charred bit that is her brother. But it isn't anyone to her, it is that burnt.

It is everyone to her.

The man's ears hurt him. He has held them under the water so long, under the roar of the fire and water, that the roar flows inside, that the sirens sing on both sides of his head, beckoning.

There are no whisperers.

There are no others.

He spreads his arms. From behind I see he makes a cross, that open angle on the arms and head, that thin dividing torso. I also see idol, the hat worn in the place where idols are kissed, where they get worn with kisses and then tinned—if not silvered. But I am not offended, despite the god stance. Misunderstandings define Me. I let them progress, I let idols wear themselves out and when they're drawn or quartered or gutted or sealed in a tomb, I benefit. I get all the credit.

He walks upstream, his arms so outstretched it is as if to put his arms around the water, he walks into it up to his waist, up to where his stomach begins with its umbilicus of metal, and he lays face down in the water.

Not ear down—face.

The hat floats off.

She sees the thin hair and the man and the man's armor and his back and his hat that now skims between the river's banks, that is now tumbling, the hat taking in the river with a gulp, the hat now sunk and skidding along the bottom into branches, into whatever else has sunk. But she doesn't run to fetch the hat.

She doesn't lean down and touch the last bubbles of the man either.

It is just a hat, just a man.

She has not been confused by the man's eyes or the metal he carried or the huge animal of his that died so wildly, so large and long-faced. She is a child and everything is possible, nothing is confusing. What confusion she does have is fear mixed with disgust, a feeling that makes her not want to step toward where he now parts the water, releasing his offal.

She sits beside the burnt bits and looks away the one way there is—up. She sees the man's eyes overhead, all blue, quite blue, an accident of a man and a woman, as all birth is accident, as unruly as the moment of making whatever it is you get, and it is just blue sky.

He is soon gone, his body loosed and tumbling after his hat but she doesn't see this. She waits until this must be so, until she can walk out into the water and it is only water, which she washes in.

The fire draws the women from the village. They cover the distance by midafternoon, meeting those who have fled. Smoke still rises in wisps that the wind twists in the slant light when they arrive and find the dead, so many and so burnt, coiled and thrust in out-of-the-body agony. The women wail, the women wrap what they find in cloth bundles and wail, the women blacken themselves, rolling on the ground and wailing, and come to wash at the river and find her. She is curled low beside the burnt bits she thinks are her brother's.

At first it is a miracle. They exclaim and run their hands over her. That she lives is a sign she has indeed been with god. But where is this god? Burnt? He is not any good as a god if he burns.

She points to the sky. He rose into the clouds, she says. See that blue there? she says. His eyes. I have all there is of him now. Inside me.

They help her out of the burnt field. Her feet keep catching on what's left of the twisted grass so she stumbles and stumbles again. My brother? she asks. She doesn't want to leave without him. But they push her on. They want to be well away from that place with its darkness, with the less-burnt outlines left from the collected bits.

Home, the women feed her and wrap her feet and her belly in leather. It is her belly that they wrap most, and she lets them. She lets them do what they must from what they know. With a god they are less sure than their own, so they wrap her well. They rub fat on her as she fattens, and fat where the dry winds cut, fat all over where her tears dry. They show her the green shoots that rise up after an afternoon of rain—green in the black stubble of the grass—and they touch these shoots to her belly.

Their grief releases as her belly swells.

But no one knows her brother's end. Of all the men who ran down the river or ran out with the rabbits or were found wandering the next day, none were her brother. She grieves over the burnt bit she chose before, a bundle short of bone and not quite a person, the one which is in fact most of him. She scars her face with rock points and wails over that bundle. But when she tries to scar her belly, the women stop her. They tell her, you will bear us this god.

She bites the woman who holds her shoulder, she bites her to the bone, then she wrests that shoulder free and takes up the rock again, aiming it again at her belly.

All the women surround her. They force her arms and legs

into nooses like the one the boy birds wear, only this time they tie the belly loop to the ground.

God must be kept out of the sky.

But at the first stirring, she eats the honey they lay out for her. And when they release her, she plants beans, she winnows the flat stalks of grain and pounds food. She has no one in her family left to feed but herself. Tall Pigeon Eye is just as dead as her brother, away so long. Her body rounds anyway, it lengthens too, she grows into a woman but they won't have her with them. She walks apart from them.

When she is ready—her screams of *Donde? Donde?* in another language are just screams to the women—she glances down in her agony and sees the head, the eyes open and slate the way they all start, and she has a moment of happiness: the squat head is surely her brother's.

Slate-colored eyes show they come from god, there's that much blue. It is a color close enough to blue that the women cluck and say nothing. But they don't bring out food or paint their faces—they wait.

The baby is rolling over by himself by the time Tall Pigeon Eye escapes from the leg irons the metal-hatted men fit him with. He gets so thin he can't keep them on. Not really. Once in a while an incarnate gets annoyed and slips out of his sentence on earth by performing a miracle. They do have to keep moving. People then explain away the miracle, they say, Remember how thin he was? Tall Pigeon Eye walks back through the tall grass talking to himself in the language of the armored men, although he doesn't realize he's picked it up until he's in the village and nobody understands what he says in his grief over his son.

It is later when he tells them in their words about carrying loads on his head and the steel collar. He doesn't tell them whether it was god with his fire who killed so many in the grass or if god will still kill them with other fire. He doesn't tell them how many of these gods come with their fire in guns, they who come by water, that water she feared, across an ocean so much bigger than a river, a water you should be afraid of even stepping into. He doesn't want to be stoned for the truth, the way others were roasted by the metal-hatted men for saying there was no gold.

What he does try is pity for his daughter, and she won't have it.

He says, Put the baby on his back so his eyes will soak up the blue of the sky, but she snatches the baby away if anyone stands over him to check the color. It could be a dark blue, says Tall Pigeon Eye. Really, she only wants the eyes black, her brother's, her mother's. But she does try prayer in the night, she does try singing his eyes blue. She even drops a tincture into one eye that causes it to cloud, and two days of crying.

She wants the baby, eyes blue or black.

Tall Pigeon Eye talks to the women, he talks and talks to them, but he is just a man to them and this is for the women.

The women pick up stones on the morning of the boy's first birthday. She can hear them whispering *black*, *black* when she opens her eyes. She puts on the hat that Tall Pigeon Eye found lodged in a curve of the river, the hat that could be a boat or an inflamed vulva or later, smashed flat, a hubcap—but never a halo—and she wraps the baby and herself in a skin and goes out to them.

I am god because I have had god inside me, she tells them.